# ART & SEDITION

**THE LEAGUE OF UTAH WRITERS
2022 ANTHOLOGY**

# CONTENTS

# FOREWORD

LEAGUE OF UTAH WRITERS
PUBLICATIONS CHAIR
CARYN LARRINAGA

Each year, the League of Utah Writers publishes an anthology in conjunction with the annual Quills Conference. It is my pleasure to present this year's anthology, *Art & Sedition.*

Art is a strangely difficult concept to define. Is there anything more subjective and, at the same time, fiercely debated? Yet there is power in that nebulous space. When a piece of art hits home for someone—really connects with them on a deep level—it can be a life-changing experience. And when it connects with many people, people who are facing similar difficulties or are under the same thumb, the impact can be profound.

I'm thrilled with the wide variety of ways this group of authors interpreted both "art" and "sedition." No two pieces are alike. Each of them have already left their mark on multiple people, from the writers who crafted them to the judges who selected them and the editors who shepherded them into their final form. And now that they're in your hands, I'm confident these works of art will leave their mark on you as well.

# ART & SEDITION

*"The artist in our time has two chief responsibilities: (1) art; and (2) sedition."*

EDWARD ABBEY

# FREEDOM THROUGH FRIVOLITY

## MARGOT MONROE

D anae pulls the lace from her neck as she cuts the corner of the crosswalk, heading toward home and Nina. Everything is oppressive today: the sticky summer haze trapping the humidity, the shimmers rising from the street when traffic isn't zipping by, and the insidious spread of the regime. She sighs and wipes at her forehead with the back of her hand.

The six-pack's cardboard handle digs into her fingers. She sighs, shifting the ginger ale from one hand to the other, then wipes at her forehead again with her newly freed hand.

"Ma'am."

Danae looks up to see a cop approaching. Perspiration rushes to her skin. She'd pulled away the crocheted lace shawl from her skin just in time to keep it from getting damp.

"Hello, Officer."

He was a young punk kid, a touch older than her daughter, just one of the students racing about back when girls were still allowed to go to school. Now he wears his uniform like a shield, untouchable and above the laws he proudly upholds.

His mirrored sunglasses successfully intimidate her, obscuring his eyes.

"You didn't stay in the crosswalk. That constitutes jaywalking. Do you realize that?"

Danae shakes her head. "I didn't, I'm sorry. My husband couldn't escort me, or he'd have kept me from breaking the law. I was just picking some things up for my daughter. She's been sick." She holds up the ginger ale as proof. And neglects to mention that she's been a widow for six years, but still wearing her ring, marking her as another man's property.

"What's wrong with her?"

"She's caught a little flu. Of course, as her mother, I'm going to take care of her."

The cop steps closer. "Why are you dressed like this if you're out running errands for your sick daughter?" He narrows his eyes at the knotted lace over the divot between her collarbones.

Danae tries to stop herself from smoothing it and fails. It is damp with sweat.

"A touch of frivolity, Officer? I spend so much time caring for my family. I'd also like to look nice for the community. And especially my husband."

He raises a skeptical eyebrow, then snorts. "You realize this is why women lost the right to vote, right? Your priorities of surrounding yourself with frivolities showed people with more sense that you needed to be cared for, and that's what we've done. We couldn't let you make our society's priorities crocheted lace." He gestures toward the shawl, then says, "Whoever made that could have been doing real work, something of value to the community. Instead, it's just a tacky bit of decoration."

She pushes back the rage before it can choke her. "And we thank you for taking care of us."

Danae's anxiety peaks as he studies her face. She isn't sure how sincere that sounded, but a cowed, stupid woman would be free to go more likely than a defiant one. Danae just needs to get back to Nina. It doesn't matter how at this point.

"I'm pleased with your gratitude and understanding."

"Definitely." More sweat slicks her forehead. She shuffles toward home, just enough to signal that she wants to leave.

His eyebrows knit together. She hasn't been dismissed yet, and he wants her to know it.

"Please, sir. My daughter really has not been feeling well." Danae wonders if acting helpless and asking for his advice would help. "Do you know of any doctors that would see her?"

He shrugs. "I don't know who would help a woman. Not much money to be made there."

"Can I please go back to my daughter? My duty is to my family, and they're my top priority."

He tips his head to the side, still watching her. Danae swallows.

"If I give you a ticket, would you be able to pay it?"

"Just barely. But if my Nina gets worse, then..." She bites her lip and looks down, relieved not to worry about the emotions on her face for the moment. This cop literally holds life and death over her, and the white-knuckle grip on her emotions is slipping.

"Will you at least *try* to be careful?" He sighs. "You're lucky I was here to let you know not to jaywalk."

Tears fill her eyes, making the cop blurry. Her hand shakes as she wipes at them. "Thank you, sir, so much. Thank you for taking care of a woman like me."

"If our job is to be caretakers for those weaker than ourselves, that's exactly what we'll do. We couldn't expect you to know better, so how could I hold you to such a high standard?"

Danae puts her hand over her heart, feeling the wild beat beneath her fingertips. The gesture looks like gratitude, but Danae wants to feel her heartbeat slow.

"Will you watch where you're going now?" the cop says. "Please?"

The 'please' almost has a flirtatious edge to it.

Danae watches herself nod in his mirrored sunglasses.

"Good." He looks down the street. "Now, do you need help getting home? Can I carry that ginger ale for you?"

"I'm almost there and know the way. I'll be careful. Thank you, Officer."

Her hand curls into a fist over the knot. The lace feels like a talisman, grounding and comforting.

He smiles and gives her a nod of dismissal.

A harried smile is the best she can give him, and she hurries down the street. She looks back after turning the corner, making sure he isn't following her, and when she's sure she's alone, she breaks into a run.

Danae bursts through the back door, startling Nina into dropping a bag of trail mix on the floor.

"What the hell, Mom?" Nina studies her mother's face. "Are you okay? What happened?" She shuffles through raisins and peanuts toward her mother, taking the ginger ale and setting it on the counter.

"We need to leave. Tonight." Danae leans back, peeking through the backdoor window to see if she was followed. "I got stopped by a cop."

Nina's eyes widen.

"I cut the corner of the crosswalk and he stopped me." Danae's fingers shake so much she can't untie the lace from around her neck.

"Let me." Nina holds her shoulders, and Danae relaxes into her daughter's care. "He didn't search you?"

Danae shook her head. "Why would he? I'm just some frivolous empty-headed woman."

"You did it. My God, you did it." Nina leans forward and holds Danae as tightly as she can. "Thank you."

Danae draws a deep breath, then says, "Okay, we need to get ready."

"You're right." Nina works at the knot of lace, gently picking it apart, then spreads the fabric triangle on the table. The shawl makes a beautiful contrast against the dark wood. Danae's anxiety kept her from looking at it earlier, but now the craftwork dazzles her.

Danae traces a fingertip along the lace trail, pointing out safe havens and turns on the crocheted map. The river was worked in a silk thread with a slight sheen to it. Tiny trees of the forest. Meadows with flowers and grass. And then: *safety*. People helping people and still doing it with beauty. Danae wonders how many necks and shoulders this shawl has graced.

"How are you feeling, honey?" Danae asks.

Nina looks up from studying the cream-colored map.

"Tired. I haven't puked, but…" She shrugs. "But it doesn't matter how I feel. I'm not ready to be a mother, and even if I was, there's no way I'd raise a child here." She drops her eyes. "You're not mad at me? You don't want to be a grandma?"

Danae laughs softly. "I'm your mother. I only want the best for you. And that's what you want for yourself and any children you'd have. So that is *exactly* what I want. I'd love to be a grandma, but first of all, I'm your mom and—" The stress of the afternoon catches up to her and exacerbates the swirling emotions into a maelstrom. Danae touches her daughter's chin, pulling her face up a little. "All I want is for you to be safe and happy. I should have done this a long time ago, but I didn't think things could change this quickly. I'm sorry I didn't do more and get us out in time."

Nina takes a deep breath. "All we can do is make the world better. We'll start with making the immediate world of our family better, then work from there." She touches the shawl, reverence slowing her breath. "Grandma taught me how to crochet. I'll make one of these too. I can't believe how beautiful this is, the care and the craftwork." She laughs again. "I might have to make more than one. I certainly couldn't make this on my first try."

Danae tries to stop her soul from shaking, stop the guilt lapping at her feet. The slide into authoritarianism was so gradual she didn't realize what was happening until it was too late. And now her poor daughter faces the hardship.

"Okay, let's finish packing so I can rest before we set out. We'll leave at sundown."

The next generation can make the world a better place, but only if they have the freedom to do so. Danae watches her daughter, watches the future, and pledges to do her part to make it safe again.

# A LAST AND FINAL WILL

## A SISTER AGATHA STORY
### BRYAN YOUNG

B rother Dominguez enjoyed his dreamless sleep, finding it most refreshing. The things he'd seen in his travels with Sister Agatha had given his nightmares far too much fuel.

He thought he was dreaming when the elderly shield maiden rousted him from his slumber and bade him come with her, but he did as he was told. He didn't know what they could do in such a bizarre case, but she always had a nose for places where a difference could be made, and he wondered if it wasn't some sort of magic or sixth sense. It was by the small hours of the night they traveled from one side of town to the other, keeping to the shadows on wet streets, traversing through alleyways all the way up and around to the bastille on the edge of the city of Copperton. The city was unusual for a number of reasons, but chief among them was that it was the first in Argonan that Brother Dominguez had been to that was not named after a saint. Every single one paid honor to a patron saint of some sort, but not Copperton.

Copperton was a mining town, and not one of the churches or saintly orders had established it. The East Argonian Mining

Concern had built it up around the nearby copper mines, and they did not afford all the comforts of the rest of the cities and towns across the realm. They also did not seem to worry about the culture of a place: their goal was to extract the precious metals and ores, and anything beyond that was outside of their care.

Darting through another alley, Brother Dominguez followed Sister Agatha up to a darkened doorway beneath an impressive arch of stone quarried from the copper mines. The company made the Order buy the stone for their own bastille, brick by brick, as though it had not been a benefit to them and to everyone.

"This way," came a voice in the dark.

Sister Agatha led him toward the voice and the door.

The door opened, and dim torchlight spilled out, revealing the speaker: a bastille guard dressed in traditional shield maiden attire of the order of St. Anselmo, replete with a spear tied to her back.

Brother Dominguez rushed into the corridor behind Sister Agatha, and the shield maiden closed the door behind them. Safe inside, Sister Agatha walked side by side through the corridors with the shield maiden, while Brother Dominguez covered their back.

"Thank you for your help, Sister Saint," Sister Agatha told the much younger shield maiden.

"It is the least I could do when I heard you were in these parts. I hope you can save his life."

"Brother Dominguez and I will do what we can," she said, nodding back in Dominguez's direction.

Brother Dominguez nodded at the bastille's shield maiden. "Greetings, Sister Saint. And this is what Sister Agatha does. If he is innocent, she will get to the bottom of such truth."

They turned a corner in the corridor and came to a staircase spiraling downward.

"He's maintained his innocence the whole while," the shield maiden said, "but he refuses to say anything in his defense. I know in my heart he is innocent, but I cannot understand why he will not help himself."

"Who is he?" Brother Dominguez asked.

"A rabble-rouser and a troublemaker, some say. He claims his real name is Hagglund, but he works by the name of Underhill and goes by that."

Sister Agatha had the keenest mind that Brother Dominguez had ever seen, and he could practically see her etching each of these details into the steel trap of her mind. "And who is it he is said to have killed?"

"The feed store owner, a man named St. Arling, and his clerk were killed in a robbery. The assailant was masked in red and was stabbed in the process. Underhill arrived at a barber-surgeon the evening of the murder with a stab wound, needing it sewn shut, and a red kerchief in his pocket. It made him the most likely suspect."

They descended one more staircase and found themselves in a dungeon of some sort. Torches lit each cell, and there were windows only on one side. The acrid soot stung Brother Dominguez's eyes, and he had to keep from coughing.

"And who is the authority here in this town?" Sister Agatha asked.

The shield maiden sighed as though it were a sore subject. "The East Argonian Mining Company is the technical authority. They allow us to operate the bastille, but they control the courts and constabulary. And they want to kill him by sundown on the morrow."

Sister Agatha paused at the edge of the cells and turned to

the shield maiden. "Why are they so keen to kill him, and so quick as well?"

"As I said, he is a rabble-rouser."

Sister Agatha furrowed her brow. "It has to be more specific than that."

"He's an itinerant bard. His songs inspire the miners. They seek their profits and, frankly, exploit their workers. He dares to oppose that."

"Ah," Sister Agatha said, as though that answered everything. "May I ask another question?"

"Of course, Sister Saint, anything to help."

"Why are you so keen to help him?"

The shield maiden set her jaw tightly. "I dislike injustice."

Sister Agatha nodded. "As do we all."

Brother Dominguez wondered if the injustice she spoke of was against all of the workers or just the man accused.

"He's right here. This way." The shield maiden led them halfway through the hallway and opened a thick wooden door with creaky black hinges and a crossbar thick enough to prevent any escape attempt by force.

Underhill sat on his bed, but even folded up on top of it, Brother Dominguez could tell he was a very tall and lanky man with hair the color of straw, small eyes, and a strong chin. He was young too. Perhaps twenty-five or thirty summers at the most. The way he held his side with his broad working-class hands gave Dominguez the distinct impression that was where he had been cut.

He looked over to the shield maiden, exasperated. "It's still like I told you, my lips are sealed forever and for now."

The shield maiden waved a hand to indicate Sister Agatha. "This is Sister Agatha of the Order of the Sainted Mother visiting from the capital."

Underhill's ears pricked up and so did his posture. "*The* Sister Agatha?"

"You've heard of me?"

Underhill tried smiling and sitting up, but the pain of his wound turned his face into a grimace. "They sing songs of your deeds from here to St. Sebastian. I'd wager a day's fair wages that you're more famous than I." He looked around and up, as though he saw a noose right there in the room. "Until they're through with my page anyhow."

Sister Agatha tilted her head. "The shield maiden here believes in your innocence. Why do you not defend yourself?"

"A matter of honor, Sister Saint, but not of mine. Honor's an overrated concept if you ask me, but I'll honor the wishes of the party of the third part. I tell many stories, but my part in this one's not mine to tell."

"You dislike honor so much but are so honorable that you'll die for the cause of another?"

Underhill shrugged.

The torchlight danced in his eyes, and he moved his head as though he were setting his words to music.

Sister Agatha must have divined something because her head cocked like a curious bird. "Who was she?"

Underhill's smile returned through the pain. "You won't catch me there, Sister Saint. They've already caught me here, and there's no use anyhow. It's all a done deal, as done as the life of St. Argon and twice as useful."

"But you maintain your innocence."

"Truly. I don't own a horse and brook no troubles with those who truck in dry tack. This St. Arling and his clerk were working-folk like the miners and have no quarrel with me or any of mine who work there. I wouldn't hurt or steal from anyone undeserving."

"It was a company store," the shield maiden said.

Underhill's brow furrowed. "In any case, I'm innocent. There's no way I'd go into a feed store, even for a cent. As I said, I haven't got a horse."

"And what of being stabbed?" Sister Agatha asked.

Underhill clutched a little tighter at his side. "It was… a misunderstanding."

But he said nothing further.

"She is trying to help you. Do you want to die?"

"Who wants to die at all? I want to live forever, but as long as my songs don't die, then at least some part of me shall live beyond. There's power in a union through a song."

Brother Dominguez found the man's manner of speech dizzying but lyrical in a way he found astounding. Was this how all those who plied their trade as songsters and bards sounded? Dominguez certainly didn't know and wondered if he would ever find out.

"I will do what I can to help you, but it would be much easier if you aided me in my quest."

"I cannot, Sister Saint, though I wish I could. It would cause a scandal, ugly and misunderstood."

"You will help him then, Sister Saint?" the shield maiden asked, as though she had a stake in the outcome, which Brother Dominguez found rather curious.

"As I said, I will do what I can."

———

Brother Dominguez folded his arms in front of himself as he and Sister Agatha walked across the village green. He knew better than to guess what Sister Agatha was thinking, working to save a man who so clearly would not save himself. But like the shield maiden who had summoned them, she despised injustice. "So, where do we start, Sister Agatha?"

"We find out who she is."

"She?" Brother Dominguez wondered if her bait had hooked more fish than he realized.

"The woman he's protecting. It's right there plain as day. She will be his alibi, if only we find the way."

Brother Dominguez scoffed. "You're speaking like him in rhyme now?"

Sister Agatha did not return the smile. "I suppose I am. I've a habit of mirroring the speech and accents of those I'm questioning. I hardly notice anymore. It helps brook trust."

"Aye," Brother Dominguez said. "But where do we start the search for this woman? It seems a needle in the proverbial haystack."

"We start with those who knew him well and find out who he saw."

"We haven't a lot to go on."

"He'll have taken residence in the worker's camp. You heard the shield maiden say he was itinerant. They'll have known him because he played for them, and we can begin asking our questions there." A bell tolled in the distance announcing the late hour. Sister Agatha turned her head in the direction of the pealing and clenched her jaw. "Time is short, Brother Saint. Speed is of the essence."

"Of course."

The trek to the encampment was a difficult one for Brother Dominguez. Copperton was built on a hill on one side and the open pit of the mine on the other. The miner's camp was down in the pit. The better to keep the workers close to the work they had to do, he supposed.

The path was a wide circle around the mine, and it was much deeper than it looked by all appearances. They took sure-footed mules down, borrowed from the abbey by Sister Agatha without permission, though Brother Dominguez knew that if they had rousted the Abbess, her permission would have been granted.

"No sense in bothering her for a conclusion easily forgone," Sister Agatha had said.

As they descended, Brother Dominguez worried that the mules would slip in the mud and send them tumbling toward their death in the chasm of the mine, or that he would fall asleep and lose his balance. Neither happened, of course, but Brother Dominguez could be a very nervous fellow. As an initiate who had been drafted by Sister Agatha, he had spent his time in monastic school studying to read books in a monastery. Traveling the realm and studying murders and human nature and making his way into pit mines on narrow roads in the middle of the night by mule was never how he imagined spending his days earning his rope and sword.

The camp itself was quiet, and by the time they made it down, the sun had begun to cut a dark line of a silhouette against the edge of the mine above as the black sky turned lighter. The entire shanty looked run-down and old. Second-hand, almost. Mud and muck filled the streets, and filth was everywhere. The surroundings were horribly poor, and he wondered how its residents could rest and recuperate from the back-breaking labor of the mine under such conditions.

Life in the encampment only began to stir when a cock crowed. Brother Dominguez began to catalog the smells as Sister Agatha had taught him to do. Smells stirred the memory, she said, and could tell a lot about a place. Aside from the standard stench of dung—from horses and humans—he smelled coffee brewing and eggs sizzling on pans over fires. The thick, woody smoke mixed with the foul odor of bodies accustomed to the stench of their own sweat, a symphony of foul odor competing for attention.

Sister Agatha led the pair of them through the encampment, looking over things here and there and muttering to herself.

"What is it you are looking for, Sister?"

"He would have stayed somewhere on the edges." Indeed, she had kept them on the fringes. "His hands were too delicate for a miner but calloused from his lute. Ah, here we are…"

Indeed, Sister Agatha had found an empty shanty behind a makeshift stage. Rocks and tree stumps made for seats in a semicircle around a firepit at the stage's foot. "This is where he would have spent his time," she said, and it made perfect sense to Brother Dominguez. "Let us see what we can spot."

The contents of his shanty had already been turned about, most likely by the company constabulary.

Sister Agatha knelt down beside the overturned desk and lifted up a mess of parchment and started reading them in turn. "He has good penmanship."

She handed Brother Dominguez a stack of papers to rifle through on his own. "I know I seek clues, but is there anything in particular you wish my eye to see?"

"Just let me know anything that crosses your mind as you read," she said, stoically reading papers of her own, angling them toward the window's morning light.

The bard's poetry was quite good to Brother Dominguez's eye, though he could see why the company would want him killed. "Here's one verse," he said aloud, reading to her from Underhill's elaborate cursive. "Come all ye workers, from every land, come join our grand industrious band, then our share of the profit we'll demand. Come now, do your part, make a stand."

"It certainly advocates a point of view. And there is definitely power in a song." Sister Agatha nodded her head. "This is interesting too, though."

"What is that, Sister Saint?"

She held up a small, leather-bound book full of pages soaked in the ink of Underhill's quill. "Hildy," she said matter-of-factly.

"Who is Hildy?"

"She's the one we're looking for."

Brother Dominguez looked perplexed—*was* perplexed. She had picked up some of the writings of a songwriter and bard and somehow jumped to that conclusion.

She smiled politely. "Come now, Brother Dominguez, you're sharper than that. This whole calfskin-bound book, expensive for a man living in a shanty on the edge of a mining community, is dedicated to poems and songs about a woman named Hildy. There is not a single protest anthem or tune to the downfall of the East Argonian company in here. If he is binding his lot up in the dishonor of honor and worried about what really happened as it might affect others, this seems to be the person he cares of the most. It stands to reason it's this Hildy."

"And what if he changed her name? Bards are known to do that, to change the names to suit a rhyme."

She nodded her head, actually pleased with his answer. "That is well thought out, and I grant you that could be the case. But at that point, the book would be filled with different names for different rhymes. And it would be a name easier to insert into stanzas than Hildy."

Brother Dominguez bowed to her and her superior intellect. "Fair enough, Sister Saint."

"So, we find her. She is the key to all of this."

She never failed to make him marvel at how her brain worked. And as much as he tried to keep up, she always appeared one step ahead of him. And she always seemed so certain of it.

"Have no fear, Brother Dominguez," she said as though she

read his thoughts as easily as Underhill's meanings in the book. "In time, you will learn to see all of this as I do. I have no doubt of that. And we *will* save this life."

————

Hildy, it turned out, was not far away.

After asking around the camp, they found that Hildy's family built the shanty Underhill had been lodging in. They had built many of the rough shanties in the encampment and lived just a few doors away from the shanty Underhill called home—temporary or otherwise.

Naturally, Hildy had no interest in speaking to Sister Agatha or Brother Dominguez and left the thin scrap of a wooden door on her shanty closed.

"I have nothing to say," she called out through the door.

"This man's life hangs in the balance," Sister Agatha said. "He clearly cared for you, even if you do not now care for him."

A quiet pause permeated between the two. Brother Dominguez had seen it before: a battle of wills between Sister Agatha and her quarry. Sister Agatha waited until the tension grew and doubled, then waited until it would have snapped beyond the breaking point for a lesser will.

"I can wait all day," the investigating shield maiden said. "But he can't."

With the silence broken, it took a moment for the tension to once again increase enough for Sister Agatha's tactic to work.

But it did.

The door opened slowly. Perhaps Hildy felt sheepish about it? Brother Dominguez wouldn't know until they went inside. They weren't exactly invited in, but Sister Agatha stepped in anyway, and he followed her.

Hildy was a young woman, twenty or twenty-five summers at the most. She looked sturdy enough to work in the mine if she needed to but delicate and lovely enough to be an object of the muse for someone like Underhill. Instead of a dress, she wore dungarees like one of the miners in the camp and a shirt with the sleeves rolled up. The work clothes did nothing to hide her feminine shape. Her hair, flaxen and long, was pulled back and pinned up to keep it out of her eyes. Hildy's face boasted a smudge of dirt interrupted with tracks from tears. It was likely she was mourning the pending death of a beau. In her countenance, Brother Dominguez detected a profound sadness that filled the room.

"What?" she finally said to her visitors.

"I am Sister Agatha of the Order of the Sainted Mother. The shield maidens of the bastille asked me to investigate because they believe Underhill is innocent."

"He is, but there is nothing I can do about it," Hildy said.

"Surely there is," Brother Dominguez said. "Sister Agatha has had great success in proving the innocence of those on death's door in cases very much like this. Albeit she often has more time to do it."

"They mean to kill him today," Hildy sobbed.

"Indeed," Sister Agatha said. "Which is why we must work quickly. Why do you say you cannot help him?"

"Because I offer no alibi. When the murder took place, I was working on the workers' soup line. Too many people saw me there, and I cannot simply lie to give him one, much as I would want to."

"I understand," Sister Agatha said. Her eyes scanned across the room, looking for anything that could be useful in her pursuit. "But do you know where he was? Alibi or not, he refused to answer any of our questions, and the best I can do is investigate his day and recreate it. Perhaps I can find the proof needed to at least save his life if I can just know where he was."

"I wish I did."

"Have you spoken to him since he was detained?"

She shook her head, and the tears began again. Urgency blossomed in Brother Dominguez's chest. He knew the pain of someone who would have a loved one torn from them too soon, and if they could spare it, they should.

"Did he have enemies?" Sister Agatha asked and then thought for a moment before smirking. "I mean, enemies other than the company. Something tells me if my trail led there, they would proffer no help."

"You would be right. But..." Hildy wiped her eyes, but there was something hidden beneath them. Brother Dominguez had slowly been learning to recognize the look of a revelation. A secret about to be shined in the light.

"He was stabbed," Sister Agatha said. "Who would do such a thing to him if he was not at the feed and tack this day?"

"There was one man who might have considered stabbing him."

"Is he not as popular among the workers as he says?"

"No. They all love him. He's funny and he entertains them. No, there's one person who just... His name is Applequist. Jonathan Applequist. And he hated Jole more than anything."

"Jole is Underhill?" Sister Agatha asked.

Hildy nodded.

"What reason did Applequist have to hate Underhill?"

Hildy looked down, unable to look at either of them. She folded her arms across her heart as though she were trying to brace against it breaking.

"Hildy, if I am to save his life, I must know." Sister Agatha put a comforting hand on Hildy's shoulder.

Hildy shrank at the shield maiden's touch. Brother Dominguez read it as shame, or perhaps fear. It might have even been a combination of the two. But fear of what?

"Jonathan was in love with me. We were... We were engaged when I met Jole."

"And you called it off?"

Hildy nodded, avoiding teary eye contact in shame.

Sister Agatha drew the much taller Hildy into an embrace, and Hildy sobbed into the shield maiden's shoulder. Then, Sister Agatha's eyes met mine. "We'll find him. And we'll get to the bottom of this, I assure you."

"You'll save his life?"

"We will."

Brother Dominguez set his jaw and straightened his posture. They *would* fix this. Of course they would. That's what they did.

———

The midmorning sun had warmed the encampment significantly by the time they had made it to Jonathan Applequist's tent. It was in the midst of the encampment, mingled in with the rest of the workers. Applequist was on the later shift in the mine, so they found him resting in his cot.

"What do you want?" he said gruffly, pulling his blanket back over his shoulder.

Applequist was a diminutive man with a weak chin and three days of stubble. His hands and face were dirty, with nowhere to clean up after a day in the mine. He looked none too pleased to see a shield maiden arrive at his doorstep.

"I want to talk to you about Jole Underhill," Sister Agatha said in a firm, clear voice.

"Nope. Get out." Applequist pulled his blanket up over his

head, the closest he could get to slamming a door in their faces.

"He is going to die, Jonathan," Sister Agatha said. Her voice walked the line between comforting and angry. Brother Dominguez had been with her for a long time and knew when she had put that edge to her voice, as calm as it might have sounded, it meant she was losing her patience.

"Serves him right," Applequist said from underneath his woolen hiding spot.

"Have you tried to kill him?" Sister Agatha said.

Brother Dominguez felt his jaw drop. It was not her usual tactic to go straight to accusations. She must have really been feeling the pressure of the sands running through the hourglass. Understandable when a man's life hung in the balance.

Applequist tossed the blanket over his head and sat straight up. His beady eyes narrowed. "Who told you that?"

"Is it true?"

"I don't have to say anything to you."

"No. You don't. But it would behoove you to do so."

"Why?"

Sister Agatha took a step deeper into the tent, toward Applequist, more aggressive than Brother Dominguez had seen from her. "A man's life is at stake, Applequist. Does that mean nothing?"

Applequist flinched.

But then they were all distracted by a commotion outside. A great din of people, practically a mob, passed right around the tent on all sides. Brother Dominguez locked eyes with Sister Agatha, and she gave him a curt nod. Taking the unspoken order, he turned and looked outside the tent, pulling the flap open to peek. A sea of people swam like fish, salmon swimming upstream to the center of the camp. Shouting.

Angry. Brother Dominguez took half a step out and was almost pushed right over.

Just as he was catching his balance, Brother Dominguez was knocked right over by another miner. Sister Agatha reached down to help him up, and he gratefully took her hand.

"What happens here?" he asked her.

"They're going to kill him now."

"Who?" Brother Dominguez asked, but he knew the answer. Who else would they be killing?

"The company," the woman shot back, thinking he'd asked a different question, but it was information he wanted, none-theless.

"I see."

The initiate turned back into the tent and took a breath to speak, but Sister Agatha beat him to it.

"We heard. We have to get there now. And you," she said, turning to Applequist. "You'll be coming with us."

———

Brother Dominguez could hardly catch his breath by the time they got to the gallows that had been erected on the edge of the mining encampment down in the center of the pit. Noon approached and sweat glistened on every brow as the sun fell directly overhead, beating down into every corner of the shantytown.

"We must hurry," Sister Agatha said.

Brother Dominguez could not be sure why Applequist came with them. He had seemed reticent but now came without force or further compelling. The smug look on his face said enough to Dominguez, though.

"I think this is a mighty fine vantage point," Applequist said, planting his heels.

"We have to find the authorities," Sister Agatha said.

"By the gallows," Brother Dominguez said, pointing to them. Indeed, the shield maiden who had summoned them in the first place stood sentinel there. Beside her were the finely-clothed money changers of the East Argonian Mining concern. One wore the frock of a magistrate, and it was clear they intended to carry out the sentence there. An executioner stood in a black hood beside Underhill who, for his part, almost looked happy by the turn of events.

"I'm not going anywhere until I see it done," Applequist said smugly.

Sister Agatha heaved in a great breath, like a monster in a story with fire in her eyes, and gripped Applequist by the arm with a talon of a hand. Then, she dragged him through the increasingly hostile crowd, fighting their way to the gallows themselves. She was stronger than she looked.

Brother Dominguez followed dutifully behind them. The whole while, they each caught sharp elbows, dirty looks, and harsh words as they cut through the crowd.

"You must stop the execution," Sister Agatha said as they reached the magistrate. "I have evidence that this man Underhill is innocent."

The magistrate, a sour old man of money dressed in finery more expensive than the clothes of the entire worker camp combined, looked her up and down, took a good account of who she was, and simply laughed. "We have seen him guilty, and by the laws of this town, he shall hang."

The magistrate waved a hand, and the executioner gripped Underhill by the shoulder.

The crowd booed, and Brother Dominguez couldn't figure out if they were booing Underhill or his would-be killer.

Underhill donned a pretty smile and soothed the crowd.

"Don't mourn, my friends. That's what they want. Don't mourn. Organize!"

The executioner placed a hood on Underhill.

Sister Agatha stepped forward, trying to intercede, but the guards at the edge of the gallows dropped their long halberds to bar her interference.

As they strung him up and from beneath the hood, Underhill began to sing, loud and strong and proud.

> *"Come all ye workers, from every land,*
> *Come join our grand industrious band…"*

The crowd's voice unified into one booming melody and they joined him.

> *"Then our share of the profit we'll demand.*
> *Come now! Do your part, make a stand!"*

That's when the executioner pulled the lever.

Underhill's voice stopped as his neck cracked, but the voices of the crowd carried on, a motley chorus of voices in three different keys. They all knew his words even though Underhill had been robbed of the ability to sing them for himself.

> *"Would you have beds of gold in the sky,*
> *And live here in a dirt-trodden shack?*
> *Would you have wings up in heaven to fly,*
> *And starve here with rags on your back?"*

They kept going and carried the tune even further, united together in song and spirit. Dominguez could pick out voices in the crowd, though some were now sobbing as they sang.

*"Would you have freedom from wage slavery?*
*Then join our grand industrious band!*
*Would you from misery and hunger be free?*
*Then come, do your share, lend a hand!"*

As the chorus swelled, even Applequist shed a tear, watching the last bits of life kick out of Underhill.

*"Come all ye workers, from every land,*
*Come join our grand industrious band...*
*Then our share of the profit we'll demand.*
*Come now! Do your part, make a stand!"*

Their voices together, singing as one, filled Dominguez with awe. The tears turned to anger, though. Anger took over. They were no longer a crowd but a mob.

He didn't have time to take in the sight. Sister Agatha yanked him backward. "Brother Dominguez, I believe it's time we left."

When the picks and hammers came out, Brother Dominguez did not argue.

———

Brother Dominguez stood beside Sister Agatha at the lip of the pit mine, looking down at the encampment and East Argonian Mining Company buildings, all ablaze. It seemed unlikely that the miners would be working for the company any time soon.

"We have lost," Sister Agatha said. "But I wonder if Underhill has not won something greater."

"How did he win at the end of a rope?"

"He wanted to die," Sister Agatha said. She extended a hand across the chaos that had been wrought beneath them as though it were obvious. "Just as there is power in workers banding together, there is power in the songs of a martyr."

"I see."

"They will live long after he does. Longer now."

"I still wish we could have saved his life."

"So do I, Brother Dominguez. So do I."

*Author's Note: The song sung at the funeral was adapted from "There is Power in a Union," a traditional folk song written by labor activist Joe Hill. The crowd sang it at his funeral after he was killed by the state for a crime he didn't commit.*

# HOLY LIGHT

## JOHNNY WORTHEN

This time the student didn't beg when the faceless guards burst into his cell and slapped the black bag over his head. He didn't gag at the stench of vomit. Didn't even wonder if it was his. He didn't resist when they pulled him roughly off his piss-stained cot and slid plastic cuffs around his raw and scabby wrists and tightened them. He anticipated the shove that drove him out the door and didn't even stumble.

This was resignation, complete and protective. The pain and hunger and cold and fear had all consumed him, and his energy now was elsewhere and spent. Detached, his thoughts were blank pieces of paper, sun-faded and warm. Potential for another day. A canvas, an empty stage, a sitting piano. His soul was thin and waiting, perhaps to perform again. Or not. What mattered now was it was not here. This was time to be endured and would end, eventually, one way or another, and he no longer cared how. He was spent. Surrender is peace. And since no reason had been offered to him for his being here, he'd given up on even knowing the why of it.

This time, they turned left rather than right, and here he missed a step, his ankle twisting on the cold concrete floor. Gloved hands righted him roughly, encouraged him to move forward with a hard slap to the back of his head.

The grip on his shoulder steered him to turn, and then again, and then he felt he was in an elevator. Doors closed, and the world shifted upwards. His ears popped.

Forward again and another hall. He limped on his ankle, felt his bruised soles beneath his weight from a distance. Turn, straight, turn. Wait. Pushed forward and down.

"Stand up, Mr. Neale. Turn around and back toward my voice."

The student struggled to his feet. His nose bled into the bag. He did as he was told.

His hands were cut free.

"You can take the bag off."

He raised his broken right hand and carefully pulled the sack away.

He faced a single steel chair bolted to the floor in a windowless white concrete room. Two cameras stared down at him from the two corners of the ceiling he could see. The voice behind him said, "You can sit down."

He shuffled forward while a dam breached in his mind at the sound of his name and drew him present. "I'm so glad I finally get an interview," he said. "I don't even know why I'm here. This is some kind of mistake. What do you want?"

The chair was chilly, even for him. He was surprised that after four weeks in the tomb, as he'd come to think of it, he could still shiver.

"You know why you're here," said the voice. "There's been no mistake, and we have what we want."

The student blinked and focused across the short space to a

black table and a single figure sitting behind it. He recognized the uniform as NAR, khaki camo pattern, black boots, red, white, and blue band around the hat meaning some kind of officer. A lapel pin.

"I was tortured."

"Yes," said the man. "Regrettable. Standard operating procedure. All part of the service. Nothing I could do about that."

"I don't understand?" he said.

The figure sighed and put his hands on the table. An electronic tablet came to life, sensing heat. It switched off again when it was ignored.

"You were always good about admitting your ignorance, Mr. Neale."

The voice registered then. A memory from before the coup, before the creation of the North American Republic, when he was still in school, five years ago.

"Professor? Professor Henning?"

"Colonel now, if you will. Colonel Henning, special attaché to Homeland Security."

"What... What's..." Neale's head spun, his tongue tightened feeling for words.

Mr. Henning had been the most popular professor on campus. His class, Art for the Sake of Art, had a two-year waiting list. Rumors were that students would come to Elder College from other schools just to take it. He'd taught the greats in all disciplines—music, dance, fine art, film, literature. It was said he inspired more geniuses than the muse.

"You're being purged, dummy," said Professor Henning. "Haven't you kept up on the news? We have a new order now. The NAR is cleaning house."

Henning looked younger now. When Neale had taken his

course, the man had been in his sixties and moved like he was in his seventies. Now he looked in his fifties and beamed like a man ten years younger than that. He took off his cap and placed it on the table, smoothing his short-cropped hair which didn't need it. He locked a cold stare onto the student.

Neale raised his hands, his broken hands, in a gesture of confusion. "I still don't understand. Why me? I haven't done anything. This can't be right."

"Why do you think you're special? Because you're white and male and look like the leaders? This isn't about genes, Mr. Neale. Well, not only. It's about ideas. It's about crime and punishment. Did you not have a non-networked computer in your home?"

"It's my old one. It's put away. I use the new one now."

"You know that owning an operational computer that's not accessible to the authorities via the net is a crime."

"I didn't even know it turned on."

Henning shook his head in disappointment. "What do you think you'll accomplish by lying? You know it turns on. You know it because you stored a copy of your book there just last month. A backup. Just in case. Just like I taught you."

"My book?"

"Your book. That pirate computer will get you prison, but your book gets you disappeared."

"But it's only a rough draft. No one has seen it. No one has read it."

"We've seen it. I've read it."

"How?"

"You probably should have composed it on the old computer," said Henning.

"A search algorithm found it?"

"Once I told it where to look."

"Mr. Henning—"

"Colonel."

"Colonel. Colonel Henning, may I ask you a question?"

The old professor glanced at the corner cameras behind Neale, and the student noticed two more in the other corners. Four cameras he could see, all trained on the interview.

"Sure," said Henning.

"How did you get here? You were the soul of enlightenment, showing how art frees the mind and elevates the cultured. Now you're a goddamn gestapo thought-cop."

Mr. Henning smiled. "Glad to see a little spunk in you. I thought we'd broken you."

"So had I." And he meant it. How was it now he was so upset, when faced with death a quarter hour before, he'd been calm? He said, "Would it help if I was obsequious? The torturers didn't think so."

"No. Not at all."

"You'll judge me the same either way?"

"The judging is all over. This is your exit interview. We'll get around to the confession in a moment." He touched the screen and the tablet lit up.

"But to your question," Henning said. "Opinions change. It is the sign of an advanced mind if, with new information, it can reach new conclusions."

"You sold out."

"I joined up. Times changed. This is a pivotal moment of history. The failed American experiment is no more. A new order rises, and though I understand it'll be different, and the growing pains will be... well, painful, the result more than outweighs the means. We will reap a great harvest of a new solidarity—"

"I've heard the slogans."

"Yes. Well, one must pull weeds to clear for new growth."

Neale stared at his old mentor. He'd hardly thought about Henning or that class in years, hadn't thought about school since it was forced to shut down. Those thoughts were too painful. No, that's not true. He had thought about school and Henning—the old Henning—in his book. He'd ranted in poetic prose about art and injustice, about midnight raids, public executions, book burnings, and silent disappearances, but he'd also celebrated art, the teaching of it, the learning, creating, witnessing—life as art.

It was a fiction told in the Middle Ages—the Dark Ages—about a group of monks hiding Jews and Arabs and Hindus in their abbey. They'd learn heretical languages after vespers to read forbidden texts by night, and then by day would preach to the peasants the orthodox canon—a hatred of foreigners, a distrust of difference, a fear of free thought. It was an allegory, a fable, and the inquisition-like forces only looked a little like the NAR security police.

"It was well written," said Colonel Henning. "If you'd have turned your skill in a more approved direction, you wouldn't be here today."

"Then the book would have been shit."

"Probably."

He became aware of his swelling ankle and the burns on his back. His distance was gone. Fear found him cold and broken, and he said, "I can rewrite it. I can delete it."

"Already deleted. The NSA sent a sniffer worm out over the net."

"Operation Memory Hole?"

"So, you have been paying attention to recent events."

"But that was just a rumor, a bad joke on Orwell and the times."

"It's an operational algorithm. Very effective. The internet can now forget. Your story is good and gone now. You'd be interested in knowing we killed six hundred and twenty copies of it. Lots of people peeking in your computer. Let's hope none of them read it. Oh, and your three physical back-ups, not including your illegal computer, gone."

"But it was a fiction. Make-believe."

"Mr. Neale, were you really not paying attention in my class? I thought you were quite gifted then, one of my best. I thought you had genius. It's why I've been keeping an eye on you."

"I remember your class."

"Then you'll recall that I taught that art is honesty buried in lies—great art shows truth below a facade of artifice. It's how it's most effective. Art versus propaganda. Resistance hidden behind a veneer of lies—a true deception—is always more effective than plain-spoken concepts in planting seeds of sedition. Propaganda can bring action but only after art has planted its idea in the imagination. I'm sorry, Mr. Neale, your story had to go. But it really was quite good."

"There was a time when that would have meant something to me."

Henning smiled again but didn't speak. After a moment, he activated the tablet and slid it across the table. The door burst open, and an armed black-clad guard stepped in and took the pad. He walked the two steps and dropped it in Neale's hands before taking up a position behind him.

"You're confessing to sedition, intent to overthrow the state, being a communist and an atheist, also felony conspiracy, owning and operating illegal technology, sexual deviation —should clear your browser history more often—and being a sleeper agent."

"A sleeper agent for whom?"

"Whatcha got?" Henning said and smiled.

The student looked down at the screen, tried to read the words but could not. His eyes were as clouded as his mind.

"Sign at the end," said Henning. "You'll see the space. Just a thumbprint will do."

"And if I don't? Wait—don't tell me. You'll get the signature after I'm dead."

"That has been known to happen."

He touched the square and the tablet beeped and shut off. The guard took it out of his hands, presented it back to Henning, and then left the room as he'd come, the barrel of his rifle catching momentarily on the door jamb.

"Camilliana," said Neale.

"How's that?" said Henning, typing into the tablet.

"You taught Camilliana. She dedicated a symphony to you."

"Yes."

"And now you're doing this?"

"That symphony wasn't in keeping with the new order."

"How? It was music."

"The artist couldn't be separated from the art. Her politics, you know."

Neale recalled that she'd been an outspoken advocate for trans-rights, a front-line personality on the picket lines demanding the return of Roe v. Wade before the coup. He hadn't heard anything of her in years.

"She was disappeared?"

"Same as you. By me."

"You're proud of it."

"I've kept an eye on my old students. I knew what some of you were capable of."

"Steinman, Morze, Larsen?"

"They were among the first. Famous and talented. Demonstrably productive and vocally dangerous. I'm now getting around to the students who had potential but hadn't realized it yet."

"Murderer."

"I kill no one. I write orders—"

"You're human garbage."

Henning smiled again, a wry, cruel, knowing smile. "I'm an artist," he said. "Sculpture, at least the marble kind, which I think I'm most like, is a unique art form. It creates by subtraction. An artist sees the shape within the rock and removes those pieces that don't belong. Society is like that. We see a shape within a blob, it's always always been there, but to get it out, we have to remove the unwanted bits."

"You're a goddamn da Vinci making *David*?"

Henning's smile was wide and genuine. A sparkle in his eye made Neale's stomach turn. Henning took a breath and his face returned to cold. "It was a metaphor," he said.

"It won't last. You said that. You said that no political movement, no nation, no limited idea or injustice can last. You said that."

"I meant it. Everything ends. Pain passes. Good things pass too, but each will have its day, and when it's gone, by time or violence, what takes up after it will be largely determined by what survived. And what did not."

"You're trash."

"One man's trash is another man's treasure," he said.

"That's lame even for you."

"You don't remember my lessons at all, do you?"

Neale thought back. The warm days on campus. Spring. It was spring semester. He was in love with Claire, whom he'd lost touch with after the coup. He'd loved Henning's class. Guaranteed passing grade for just showing up. Lectures that invigorated and inspired. It was art appreciation on steroids, whimsical, musical, valiant, profound. Humanities in motion.

"Gertrude Stein's salon?" coaxed Henning.

"Stein had a running party in Paris."

"A salon."

Neale remembered. "Hemingway and Picasso were regulars, Fitzgerald and Pound. James Joyce. I remember you saying that great talent spurred greatness in others."

"The NAR would call that place a nest of vipers, and rightfully so. One deviant feeding off other deviants."

"And from that came *A Farewell to Arms* and *Guernica*."

"Neither one popular in certain circles."

"I don't understand why we're talking about this. I'm not—"

Henning raised a hand. "Your education with me is over, Mr. Neale. Grades are posted."

Neale stared, wondering how much the hunger, cold, and pain were contributing to his confusion. The world was upside down, had been for years, but he'd held himself together by believing deep down in the hidden hopes he saw now he'd always had, that he'd one day go back to school and finish his degree, probably harboring some dream of retaking Henning's class, just for the joy of it.

"In old Canada," said Colonel Henning, "in the middle of nowhere, there is a prison. An abandoned Cold War missile silo. A hole in the ground in a place that goes from being a frozen wasteland in winter to a mosquito sauna in summer. It makes the Gulag look inviting. It's open and empty. It has no official name. It doesn't officially exist. Some call it the oubliette; I like to call it the salon. I'm sending you there."

"You're not killing me?"

"What makes you think I'm not?"

Neale felt lead harden in his veins.

Colonel Henning pushed his thumb to the tablet, and the screen changed from white light to red. "I write orders, and sometimes people get killed because of them, but my hands are always clean."

"In school, everyone thought you had a Christ complex," said Neale with verve he didn't know he still possessed, "but it turns out it was Pontius Pilate all along."

Henning burst into laughter. "What spunk you have! Four weeks of torture and you still spit in my eye. Well done."

"You always were an inspiration."

"Thank you."

"Your ego... You ever think that maybe the torture is why I'm spitting in your eye?"

"That couldn't be helped, but no, I don't think that. You're spitting in my eye because you think you knew me. You're disappointed with the failures of your fantasy and showing it with a tantrum. You're spitting because defiance is the last act of someone who has nothing else to do. You can't bargain your way out of this."

"Have I even tried?"

"Not with me."

Neale recalled the silent torture sessions. Masked men hurting him, never asking him a single question. Never speaking at all, just hurting him, torturing him. Waterboarding and electric shocks. They'd hung him upside down, frozen him with ice water, burned his legs with cigarettes, his back with a cooking torch. How he'd begged to tell them what they wanted to know, to do what they wanted him to do, to be anyone they wanted him to be to make them stop, never to get an answer.

Henning said, "Mr. Neale. You'll live a while longer. *Dum vita est spes est.*"

"You're killing me slowly."

"Would you prefer a green plastic bag in a Cambodian rice patty?"

"No," conceded the student.

In a softer voice, even consoling, Henning said, "We're all dying, son. Fast or slow. What matters is what we do with the time we have."

The student's mind, though foggy from rage and hunger, pain and fear, churned with new malice and energy at the thought of the evil this man had done, how he'd raised a generation of artists only to extinguish them now.

"Not all of them…" said Neale, tears finding his cheeks. "Right? Not all of them?"

"Say again." Henning raised one hand and the door opened. Two guards came in.

"Lily Patrick, the poet," said the student as guards approached. "Morales the painter, Jackson Harret—he won an Oscar. Mentioned you in his speech. And that one girl who could sing *The Fifth Element* song."

"That was Amanda Lee," said Henning. "All gone before you. And Marsha Sodovich, the dancer, Ahamdi the calligrapher, and even that mime, Phillips, from your class—remember him?—all gone now."

Neale heard his heart in his inner ear, felt new blood drip out his nose. "I haven't the words to describe what I think of you, Colonel Henning."

"More writer's block, huh? Well, maybe you'll think of something before the end."

The guards lifted him by his wrists. Neale felt his scabs break open and ooze as they bent his hands behind him and cinched plastic cuffs.

On came the bag again.

The same bag; blood and vomit and all.

Now he resisted as they marched him away. He screamed obscenities and kicked at the legs of the guards. He spun out of their grasp, and when he was pulled back, his head slapped and punched, he took the pain as incentive to try harder.

Just as he felt a needle stab into his thigh, the moment before unconsciousness, he thought he heard Henning laughing behind him, "Keep it up, Mr. Neale," and he was out.

———

When his senses returned, he was inside a box inside a plane. His hands were unbound. He was shoeless in an orange jump-suit. The box was steel and cold and tall enough to sit in but not stand. With light from one of the air holes, he found a box of crackers and a bottle of water. These he consumed immediately only to regret it just as quickly.

What was it Henning had said? *Dum vita est spes est.* It was one of the few Latin phrases he knew. It meant, roughly, 'as long as there is life, there is hope.' A taunting jibe that Neale took to heart, finding hope of surviving by hoping for revenge.

There was a collar around his neck. He could feel a padlock on the back of it. Hanging from the front, like a literal dog tag, was a heavy plastic card with an embedded chip. For the little time he'd have left, he'd now be a number, a binary code to replace his name lest anyone remember it and him.

He shrank into a small ball to conserve warmth. Through holes the size of dimes, he saw he was in the cargo area of a large, loud plane. There were crates held to the decking with wide fabric straps under flickering fluorescent lights. He could see his breath, and he tried to slow it, to get hold of the anger welling inside. He'd warm himself with irony. It was the in-flight movie.

Henning playing Orwell. A sick joke. Henning might as well have called him Winston. Off to Room 101. The parallels were too sick. Trial by book. A journal or a fiction, what was the difference? Oh, yeah. Henning suggested the fiction was more dangerous. Bully for him.

Henning had never done anything. Never written a book or song. Never a painting or had an original thought. He taught a class; the same one over and over again. Neale laughed then, knowing the man was a failure. *He* at least had written a book. A pretty good one—so said the only person to read it. The book was gone now, but what of that? He'd written it. He'd stirred the universe with its creation. A pop in the cosmos, its existence enough to alter trajectories and move fate. It had doomed him, but it was something, and he'd spoken truth.

He remembered the hellish prison he was no doubt en route to now. The oubliette, a place to be forgotten. Or the salon. Henning's little joke on the cream of twentieth century culture. The avant-garde of their time, the mega-clique of creative energy, was just a nest of vipers.

And what was that about garbage? One man's trash... There was something there, a quip Henning had made. Something about the salon.

He remembered. Gertrude Stein had a piece of broken marble, supposedly some of the debris from da Vinci's *David*. She used it as a paperweight and a conversation starter. Obviously an apocryphal story, or Stein had been duped, but what was the lesson there?

The plane jostled and tossed him forward onto his ankle. It was good and swollen now. The pain brought out a scream.

It was answered by a harsh voice saying, "No screaming unless you want me to push you the hell out of the door."

"Where are we?" Neale couldn't see the speaker, but he was close.

"Not sure, but you're bound for the oubliette. You must be one big piece of shit to get sent there."

"Why?"

"If the world had an asshole and couldn't scratch it, that'd be the oubliette, your new home. It's goddamn *Mad Max* up there. No guards. No fence. No supply. Dog eat dog, but the dogs are all dead, so you gotta ask yourself what *do* they eat up there?"

"You don't bring them supplies? Food?"

"Just you. We'll drop you off with a nice bottle of steak sauce. Nummy nummy."

New horror found its way into the student's imagination. What worse fate was there than being eaten by people? It was something that had occurred to him in recent months among the food riots and race riots and empty store shelves and power outages. To think he'd ever pine for that life of boiled buckwheat and cheese spread. In frustration, he kicked at the hinges of the box but this only shot another bolt of pain up his leg. He screamed again, and before it had subsided, he screamed again as the box was electrified.

"I said shut up!"

When it was done, Neale's hair was singed and his jumpsuit burned. His good foot had a blister on its heel, and pain planted itself firmly in his mind and sowed seeds of despair. Sensing the danger of hopelessness, he forced himself to focus on anything else; the plane, a song, a movie—the evil bastard Henning, human trash.

That piece of broken marble. Someone had come to visit Stein's salon with the sole intent of seeing it. He couldn't remember who it was. The list of dignities who frequented 27 rue de Fleurus—God, he remembered the address!—was large and impressive. He wracked his brain but could not remember who had come. Maybe it was all of them. No matter. The idea, now he recalled it, was that the piece of rock brought certain people together. Trash and treasure. Like a seed in an incubator of greatness. The idea seemed poetic then. Now it was just pathetic.

The plane landed twice, days spent in a hangar, while Neale, hungry, hurt, and tired, warmed himself with rage and tried to sleep. No one brought him food. He had no water. His cube was foul, his resolve tested by the cramped space, rising stench, and loneliness, but he fought through it, vowing to Henning, the waste of skin, that he would indeed 'keep it up.'

The third time the plane set down was after a long flight. It could have been twelve hours. Could have been forty. Time was plastic.

It landed with a bang. The engines changed pitch, it rocked to the side, pushed by winds, he figured. It moved, taxied, and stopped. Then a blast of freezing air and murky light cut into the bay as his box was released from its straps and pushed down a ramp.

He heard it crunch into snow just under the fuselage. And then the fuselage was gone; the plane taxied and took off. He listened to the engine's roar pass and disappear, all the while watching snow leak into his box like glistening crystals of doom, changing the smell from rot to cold and coming death.

All was silent for a time while Neale wondered if it was better to freeze or be killed by cannibals.

The sound of crunching footsteps preceded his box being jostled and struck. The door was pried apart and thrown open.

"Can you move?" came a woman's voice.

Against the brilliant light of the snow-spread plane, Neale saw four figures. One was bent over and looking inside, another reached in and took his hand to lead him out. He was too weak to fight and complied. Once out, he was smothered in a blanket and hurried away.

He glanced behind as four figures pushed his steel crate off the runway to sit with a dozen like it. Before him, a dome of snow, a huge igloo with a single black door. To there they went.

The door opened with a decompressing hiss, and a warm blast of air mussed his hair under the blanket. It was a receiving room of some kind. Heavy coats and warm winter gear hung off hooks along the walls.

"My name is Camilliana," said the woman. "We'll learn who you are in a bit. You are safe now. You are saved. Welcome to the Salon."

A cleanly shaved man smelling of lilac opened his blanket and inspected his body. "Dehydration, broken ankle, hands will need resetting. Food. A bath. He'll be okay."

"Excellent," said Camilliana.

"Camilliana?" said Neale through chattering teeth. "*The* Camilliana?"

Someone unlocked his collar and handed the card to the woman, who looked like an older version of the virtuoso he remembered.

"Yes," she said and slid the card into a reader.

"You're Jerry Neale, writer," she read. "Capital crimes. Henning says you have fight in you."

"That bastard…"

"Saved your life," said a man behind him. "Didn't you hear? Capital crimes. You could be dead."

"Small mercies."

"He doesn't get it yet." The man's voice was familiar. Neale turned to look. It was Phillips, the mime from his class.

"Let's get him cleaned up and fed," said Camilliana. "If we hurry, we can still make the curtain."

"A play?"

"Jackson Harret is acting in *The Crucible* tonight. Directed by Antoine Pierre. Open mic to follow."

"What?"

"Steak or squash?" Phillips asked. He held a glowing electronic tablet.

"You have food?"

"Only enough for fifty years."

"And we're nuke proof," added Camilliana. "With more room than the Overlook Hotel, minus the bloody elevators."

The door to the outside opened and in came the figures from before. Neale recognized all of them. There was Steinman, Larsen, Ahamdi, the calligrapher, and Amanda Lee, the singer. Each was ruddy and healthy—tanned, even—and each smiled a welcome when they met his eyes with their sparkling ones.

"Can't wait to see what you have to offer us," said Steinman.

"His name is Neale. A student. An author."

"Never heard of him."

"I'm sure he'll be full of surprises," said Amanda. "Dare I say, brilliance?"

Steinman said, "Henning's never been wrong yet."

"You're just saying that because he liked you," teased Larsen.

"He liked all of us."

"Suck up."

"How many books did you dedicate to him?" asked Amanda.

"The only one that mattered was the Nobel winner," said Steinman. "...and eight others."

They laughed.

"Oh, and there's a text attachment," Camilliana said, reading the screen. "Something called *Holy Light.*"

"That's my book," said Neale.

Camilliana read: "*The monks of St. Elder met in secret to hide from the eyes that would blind them. There, in seclusion, they read poetry and relished in it. Their joy was the art itself, but their goal was to tend the creative flame that one day, when the world was right and bright again, would light a new beginning. Unseen and safe, set aside like sturdy jars of rich honey waiting in a cool and cared-for cellar, they read and danced and sang the forbidden songs."*

# ALL IN A DAY'S WORK

## C.W. ALLEN

There are moments in life you'll never forget, and your first time in the back of a police car is one of them. And by your first time, I mean mine. Which happened to be November 18, 2020, on a mountain road outside Moab, Utah.

Well, okay—it wasn't the *police* police. This was the nature police.

Fun fact: the nature police get rather grumpy if you imply they don't count as "*police* police." They are likely to inform you that Law Enforcement Rangers of the Bureau of Land Management are not only authorized to arrest people, but have access to an array of devices with varying levels of deadliness to help that process along, if necessary. Ask me how I know.

I had no desire to experience any level of deadness, so I allowed them to march me down the deserted canyon path to the gravel road. I was *not* being paid enough to secure a life-time-commitment type of devotion. Sure, the excitement of field work held a certain appeal when I took the job, but I wasn't willing to trade my life for a good quarterly performance review. My dignity, though—absolutely. Which is how I ended up in handcuffs, chatting with the nature police from the back seat of their dust-smattered off-road vehicle.

They had an awful lot of questions. I knew the answers, certainly. There were straightforward, logical explanations for all of them. But I wasn't authorized to give those answers. The employee handbook and semilunar training luncheons made that quantum crystal clear. And somehow, I doubt the truth would have made them feel any better. So, lies it was.

"Did you put that thing there?" the tall ranger wanted to know. At least that one I could answer honestly—no. No, I did not personally install a shiny metal prism twice my own height in the bare red bedrock. I consider myself pretty resourceful, but he was giving me way too much credit if he thought I could pull off a feat like that all by my lonesome.

He followed that up with the question he probably should have led with: "What *is* that thing, anyway?" I'm sure that's exactly what he asked himself the first time he caught sight of the antenna. Only the officer had no idea it was an antenna, and I wasn't about to correct him. The visibility deflectors were supposed to fill in the antenna tower's entire footprint with a reflection of the surrounding scenery. And if the deflectors failed, putting the towers in remote, uninhabited locations was supposed to buy us enough time to make repairs before anyone noticed. Just my luck the nature police had to be patrolling that exact spit of desert when I arrived to troubleshoot.

From what I could piece together from their interrogation, apparently some scientist caught an overhead view of the tower from a helicopter and asked the local nature police to check it out. And now they were running around like dodos with their heads cut off, rambling about "monoliths" and "art installations" and "alien hoaxes." They weren't going to like reality any more than their frantic imaginations, so I let them ramble.

"What happened to the sheep?" his partner demanded. Ah, well… that was unfortunate. It wasn't my fault the beast had chewed through the cable—it shouldn't have been able to see the cable in the first place, after all. Actually, it was the beast's fault I had to be here at all, so if anything, it owed *me* an apology. I was about to assure the ranger the animal was definitely dead before it had time to feel embarrassed about eating things that were both invisible and clearly not food, let alone experience any discomfort. But I decided against it, mostly because of the way she was glaring at me—as though I had some personal grudge against the wooly, crescent-horned creature. She seemed like she was probably a lot more pleasant to be around when she wasn't on wildlife-avenging duty. Someone you'd like to get a refreshing dragon fruit juice with or invite over for a nice game of Parcheesi. I felt a small prick of regret when I realized how this day was likely to end for her.

For both of them.

I settled for a shrug.

She brought up the scorch marks next and informed me that starting wildfires on federal land was a felony (with an accompanying list of applicable punishments). But once again, she was blaming me for her beloved sheep's crimes. You can't expect to chew through a fourteen-strand molecular transducer cable without shooting off a few sparks. And anyway, there wasn't any fire to speak of; the location had been cleared of any scrub brush, tumbleweeds, and other flammables before installation. Besides being enshrined in the employee handbook, this procedure was basic common sense. The equipment's reflective surface combined with the local solar radiation index was just asking for a fire to start—like taking a magnifying glass to ants swimming in napalm.

I decided we were getting off on the wrong foot. Here we'd just met, and already the rangers thought I was some kind of rock-defacing, poaching, pyromaniac nature villain. I briefly considered bringing up the dragon fruit juice and Parcheesi idea, but somehow the middle of my own arrest didn't strike me as a prime networking opportunity.

They insisted on taking down my name. I had to make something up, of course. I don't remember what name I gave them—something common and unremarkable. The tall ranger's eyebrows scrunched together funny as he wrote it down, though. I guess what passed for unremarkable back home didn't cut the mustard here, because that led him to ask where I was from. No, *ask* is the wrong word. Demand. Accuse. *Threaten.*

"You're not from around here, are you?" he said, squinting into my face with a sneer.

Ironic. He had absolutely no idea how correct that assessment was. Although I guess technically that would depend on the definition of "here." But I wasn't about to say anything that would raise even more questions.

I slapped on the most innocent face I could muster. "What makes you say that?" I asked. Was my uniform giving me away? Headquarters insisted the standard-issue jumpsuit wouldn't attract undue attention. But then, this was the first time I'd actually had to work with an audience.

His partner rolled her eyes. "You're not carrying any water. The locals all know better. It's bad enough having tourists treat everyone in Moab like 'the help' without us having to scrape dehydrated hikers off the trails as well." Her rant was really getting on a roll now. "Just last week I had some woman from Milwaukee threaten to sue the entire department for not having adequate drinking fountains installed. In the middle of the desert! I mean, c'mon lady, this isn't Disneyland."

I understood. Clients often blamed me for the problems they called me to solve. I nodded with what I hoped was a sympathetic expression, but this only seemed to make her more suspicious.

She squinted, a look of shrewd comprehension creeping across her features. "Speaking of water... you couldn't have hiked all the way to the monolith site without any. You must have driven at least part of the way. Where did you leave your vehicle? We'll have to have it towed."

As though her question had summoned them, at that precise moment the cavalry arrived. And by cavalry, I mean my foreman, along with the department manager and two security guards. And in a shocking turn of events, they were also mad at me.

They shimmered into being like the away team from an old *Star Trek* rerun beaming onto an alien planet. Maybe the security guards were thinking the same thing, because they flashed their scanners at the barren rock formations like they expected ugly bipeds in rubber masks to dart out from behind them at any moment. The department manager just stood there, arms folded, wearing a scowl that could curdle milk.

"Why aren't you answering your com link?" the foreman demanded, completely ignoring the rangers. "Your two o'clock appointment is still waiting, and I had to transfer Bludgins to pick up the slack on the rest of your schedule."

"Ran into some trouble with the locals," I explained, with a nod at my captors. "I had to leave it at the work site with my tool kit."

"Leaving your tool kit unsupervised is a level six infraction," he scolded. "I'll have to issue a demerit."

The rangers' brains appeared to be short-circuiting trying to process four people stepping out of the ether like some kind of indignant mirage. So they simply ignored the part that didn't jibe with their understanding of the laws of physics and drew their weapons. Which, naturally, led the security team to aim theirs. It might have turned into a regular Old West shootout if the rangers had been capable of moving while fixed in the blue beam of a momentum arresting ray. They could still talk, though—a necessary feature for interrogations, you see—so once they finished coughing their tongues back up, they had even *more* questions to add to the list. Boring, predictable queries like, "Where did you come from?" and "What on earth does that monolith thing do?"

My foreman rolled his eyes and sighed but finally waved at me for an explanation. "Might as well satisfy their curiosity. They won't be around long enough to tell anyone else about it."

I flashed my palms in a kind of *don't blame me* gesture. At least, I tried to—the handcuffs sort of dampened the effect I was going for. "Sorry about all this," I said. "Just trying to do my job. See, we stumbled across your transmission waves about a century ago and put up these towers to boost the signals. We figured out pretty quickly you didn't know about us and weren't a threat, but since the antennas were already in place, we kept them running so we could monitor your world from a safe distance."

"Monitor our *world?*" the tall ranger interrupted. "So you *are* aliens!"

"Well… no. We've always been here, just… not *here* here, if you know what I mean."

They didn't.

"I guess you might call it an alternate dimension?" I tried. "We occupy the same physical space, but we can't detect each other without phase shifters."

"And the monolith is one of your transmission towers?" his

partner asked. "So you can *spy* on us?" She gasped, then spit out a wild accusation: "You're preparing an invasion!"

I couldn't help it: I blushed. "Actually..." This was so embarrassing, but I'd already explained halfway—might as well let the beans out of the bag. "I hear it started as a military surveillance kind of thing, but then the officers developed a taste for your sitcoms, and the bigwigs at HQ realized they could rebroadcast the signals without having to pay royalties, so..."

That wave of dawning realization finally made it up to her eyes. "Are you saying... you're a cable repair team?"

Oh, well—so much for thinking I might be a dashing secret agent or strangely attractive extraterrestrial. I nodded.

"And we've been off the air for nearly *two hours,*" the department manager spluttered. "Wrap it up, people!"

The foreman aimed a grim nod at the security guards, who prepared to turn up the power dials on their momentum rays. At Cobalt, the rays only prevented limb movements, but all the way up to Magenta stopped involuntary processes too. Like breathing, or heartbeats, or brain synapses.

I sighed and shuffled a quarter turn in my seat so I wouldn't have to see. This was for the best, right? Company policy, after all. Nothing I could do.

But then that nagging voice lounging in my brain's back seat had to chime in. *Is that what Captain Kirk would do? Just turn away?*

*What about Superman?*

*Zorro?*

*Lucy Ricardo?*

*Lassie?*

Well, Captain Kirk would at least find a way for the adventure to end with some smooching, so maybe he was on to something. I didn't have a secret identity to put on like

Superman or Zorro, not to mention talents bordering on the impossible. Lassie would just run for help—no time for that. But Lucy... yeah, I could get behind a little strategic mayhem.

"Wait!" I blurted out.

Everyone turned.

My foreman sighed, pinched the bridge of his nose to adequately broadcast his long-suffering, then glared at me. "Problem?"

"They... uh... that is, *he* confiscated the frequency modulator I was trying to install," I fibbed. "It's still in his pocket."

He snorted. "They'll be easier to search when they've stopped resisting."

"But the momentum ray will scramble the modulator's electron paths," I lied even more outlandishly. "I mean, just think what it does to brains. It'll take three weeks to get a new one in, and I can only imagine all the angry calls you'll get at headquarters if customers have to go that long without their *Gilligan's Island* reruns."

The foreman snorted again in an excellent imitation of an irritated rhinoceros that was looking forward to trampling me later. He motioned for the security team to turn down the juice on their rayguns. I slid awkwardly off the back seat and out the open car door.

I flashed my handcuffs at them. "I'll need to get out of these before I can install it."

One of the security guards turned his ray off entirely and then plucked a rock out of the red dust. He marched up to the immobilized nature police and attempted to dislodge the keys from the shorter ranger's utility belt, tentatively prodding with the rock to avoid sticking his hand in the beam still projected by the other guard.

I selected a rock too—with my feet. "Oops!" I stumbled dramatically over it, kicking the rock in the direction of the armed security guard while careening into the other one. My shoulder caught him in the ribs and we both went down, bowling over the nature police in the process. I didn't catch the action from my place in the pileup, but since the beam didn't freeze us, I guessed my rock must have connected with a tender enough location on the first guard to make him drop his momentum ray. He didn't have time to turn it off first, so when it landed in the dirt, the blue beam shone on the feet of the foreman and department manager, trapping them in place.

I snatched the keys off of one ranger's belt and hopped up, still handcuffed, to offer my assistance to my superiors. "Clumsy me! Here, I'll get it." I picked up the momentum ray and waved it around, feigning a search for the controls. "Say, how do you turn this thing off?"

You know how a disco ball or a strobe light seems to chop time up into stuttering fragments? That's exactly what the momentum ray did, alternately freezing and releasing whoever the beam landed on as I let chaos take the driver's seat. Everyone could move a little when the beam flashed out of their way, but it came back around again before they could make enough progress to disarm me or attack each other. Using my thumbs, I twiddled the dial to Vermillion and gave the rangers one last sweep. They fell into an unconscious heap in the dust.

The security guard next to the rangers—I never did learn his name, so let's call him "Bobbert"—shook his head and propped himself up to his knees. He pulled his momentum ray from its holster only to find it smoking like burnt toast. He must have landed on it when I fell into him because it was thoroughly smashed.

I allowed myself a tiny smirk. *Oops.*

The other guard—let's call him "Jimothy"—stomped over and attempted to snatch the remaining raygun from my hands.

Too bad I was still handcuffed and trying to hold the ray and a set of keys at the same time. I dropped them both, and Jimothy and I clonked heads as we simultaneously bent to retrieve them. The collision had me seeing stars; it's not my fault I happened to tread on the raygun repeatedly as I stumbled away.

That one started smoking too.

The foreman and his supervisor huffed some more. "Great work, idiots! *Now* what are we supposed to do?"

I scooped up the key ring and dropped it into the foreman's hand, then held out my arms. He rolled his eyes but pinched the tiny key between two sausage-fat fingers and unlocked my handcuffs.

Bobbert nudged one of the unconscious rangers with his boot. "Only knocked out," he reported. "They'll be awake in a minute or two. And *now* we can't finish the job!"

"Speaking of finishing the job," I added, "I'll need to order an invisibility regulator before I can get that antenna up and running again. And a transducer cable—the local wildlife chewed through it. Should be here in four to seven business days."

The supervisor looked like her hair was about to catch fire.

"Hey, that's just facts," I reported. "Not my fault the company doesn't include them in the standard repair kit. Maybe you can lobby someone higher up the chain about loosening their purse strings a little and getting us some decent equipment."

The foreman eyed me dubiously. "I thought you said it needed a frequency modulator."

"That too." I strolled over to the nature police and pretended to fish something from the tall ranger's shirt pocket. His partner rolled to her side, snoring.

"Everyone back to the antenna," the supervisor ordered,

pointing a manicured fingernail in my direction. "You— retrieve your tool kit and com link, and we'll be on our way. You will complete the repair in a deflecting suit when the parts arrive, understood? I don't want any more locals seeing anything unusual. *No. More. Screwups.*"

I offered her a jaunty salute and a winning smile. "Yes, ma'am! Don't worry, once the antenna is invisible again, the locals will completely lose interest in this kooky 'monolith' idea."

"What about these two?" Jimothy asked, still rubbing the goose egg on his skull. "Won't they tell someone?"

"They already knew about the antenna," Bobbert argued. "A couple more days won't change anything. And besides, who'd believe them if they talked? 'People from another dimension are pirating our cable'... They'd be laughed all the way to the unemployment office!"

"Yeah, I suppose you're right," I said with a glance back at the snoring pile of nature police. "Too bad. After all, they were just trying to do their jobs."

All the other people trekking back to the antenna were as mad as wet cats, but I couldn't help smiling to myself. Sure, I'd be spending the rest of the day getting yelled at by miffed customers and impatient corporate suits alike, but my shift would be over in a couple hours. Then I could kick back with a tall glass of dragon fruit juice and relax. And I knew just how to toast a hard day's work (and my very first arrest)—with an *I Love Lucy* marathon.

# LIFE IS NOT A POEM

### TALYSA SAINZ

I.
You want those delicious plums in the icebox,
but you don't take them.
You pick those glossy purple blackberries
and eat them before they rot.
Your lover didn't brag
about their devotion to your flaws
or compare you to perfect weather.
Maybe death doesn't stop for you,
even when you want it to.
Maybe you take the path more traveled by
because not everything in your life
is a fucking poem.

We're all caged birds,
but not all of us sing.
When the light begins to die,
your rage is useless, wild, uncivil.
Perhaps every song of yourself

doesn't have a meter or rhyme
or a beautiful tune.
When the Jabberwocky comes for you,
your vorpal sword is sitting on the
highest closet shelf, gathering dust,
because you missed your call to adventure.

If no man is an island,
why do we feel so unconnected,
separated, alone,
left to fend for ourselves?
Just because you're the captain of your soul
and the master of your fate
doesn't mean you're skilled in either capacity.
Not everyone is born to be a captain.
Some of us are mere ship dwellers,
unwanted by those on land.
Sometimes you get no resolution
or fulfillment
or epiphany.

Even in your cage,
you don't have to sing
to be alive.

II.
No poetry encapsulates
the unpredictable monotony,
the unexciting routine.
No metaphorical image captures
the anguish you endure.
No allegorical journey relieves your burdens.
No rhyme gives you comfort or closure.

No alliteration connects the
disjointed hell in your head
or desires in your heart.

Patterns in your life don't fit into pentameters.
Reality doesn't fall into sonnets,
despite how effortless
Shakespeare made it look.
Walk the paths of Plath,
Hughes, Cummings, Kipling.
Find meaning in the word order,
the collection of sounds,
the assonance and consonants,
the metrical verses,
the balance of stress,
and feel ever so alone
that your life doesn't feel as
damn poetic
or magnificently deep.

Life is more than every line of poetry
stacked on top of itself.
You are bigger than Beowulf
More complex than Byron
More depressed than Emily Dickinson
More hopeless than Virginia Woolf
More hopeful than Maya Angelou
More passionate than Neruda
More contemplative than *Leaves of Grass*
Your woes are more haunting than *The Raven*
Your life more ordinary than a red wheelbarrow
on which so much depends.

Even in the ordinary,
you are more than
any poem you could fathom.

# COLORING THE GLOOM

## BROOKE J LOSEE

Eric couldn't be certain since it changed on a regular basis, but judging by the wall of lavender-colored trees, he'd guessed his daughter's favorite color for today. Leah dipped her brush—no, perhaps doused more adequately described her motions—in the pale purple paint and gave the final bare trunk a pile of oddly colored leaves. He restrained himself from mentioning the unrealistic look of the seven-year-old's depiction, an effort that grew more difficult with each painting she created.

He'd never been one to understand what many called *art*. Sure, a majestic mural of the French countryside or portrait of the *Mona Lisa* might draw his attention and garner appreciation, but deciphering the hidden meanings of abstract creations only frustrated him.

Leah gave the brush a swirl in the small cup beside her, turning the water murky, and then dabbed it into her next preferred color—a vibrant pink.

"What are you doing with that color?" he asked, wondering if today she would use it for the grass or the sun.

"Armor," muttered Leah, her gaze focused on her dainty strokes.

"Armor?"

She nodded, and Eric wasn't sure what confused him more: that her painting would feature armor or that she intended to make it pink.

He watched her for several moments before asking, "Is the armor for a knight?"

"Yes."

Leah had always been reserved like him, but her quiet demeanor had only deepened the last few months. She and her mother were close, but his wife's depression had taken a turn for the worse, leaving him to spend more time with Leah while she struggled to pull herself from a pit of despair. Eric offered his wife support as best he could, but this recent bout had taken a heavier toll.

"Do you think I could be the knight?" he asked.

Leah looked up, and her caramel-colored eyes scanned over him as if considering the request. She shook her head. "No, thanks."

Eric chuckled. "Why not? Am I not fit to be a knight?" He supposed he wasn't. Knights always saved the day, and he hadn't been able to save his wife, Eleanor.

She shrugged. "Because I'm the knight. Maybe next time."

He could hardly be upset with that response. At least she didn't think him incapable of the task. Not that his quiet desk job downtown wasn't evidence enough. Analyzing expense reports likely required less talent than fighting dragons.

Leah painted a head on top of the pink armor, one with curly brown hair, and added a set of bright-orange boots to *her* feet. She finished the ensemble by giving the knight a yellow sword—well, he assumed that's what his daughter meant for the slender stroke of paint to be.

"You know, if you keep practicing, your artwork could inspire people one day," said Eric.

Leah paused from dunking her brush into a deep red that reminded him of the brick exterior of their house. "Inspire them to what?"

Eric scratched the back of his head. "I suppose it depends on what you paint. Art has been known to inspire all sorts of things—to change the world and the way people see it."

Her face pinched with contemplation, but she stayed quiet. Leah wasn't just reserved like him; she'd also inherited his analytical nature.

Eric gave her a hug. "Daddy's going to take a shower. I'll help you clean up once I've finished."

"Okay."

Eric released a heavy sigh through his nose as he entered his room. Eleanor lay on their bed but sat up when she noticed him. "How are you feeling today?" he asked, slipping to the bedside to give her a kiss.

"A little better," she answered with a hollowness to her tone that ate at him.

"I'm glad to hear that. Can I get you anything before I jump in the shower?"

"No, I think I'll go start on dinner."

Eric took her hand and gave it a gentle squeeze. "You don't have to if you're not feeling up to it. I can throw something together once I'm done."

Her lips lifted slightly. The glimpse of even the smallest of her smiles warmed him. How long had it been since he'd seen one? He couldn't remember, and that realization only pulled at his heart.

"Thank you, but I actually *want* to cook something today," she said, patting his hand.

The admission seemed to take her by surprise as much as it

did him, lighting her eyes in a way he hadn't seen in a long time. She rose from the bed with her little smile still in place and left a soft kiss on his cheek. "But I wouldn't mind some help once you're done."

"I'd love to help. I'll be quick."

Eleanor nodded, and as she made her way into the hall, hope swelled inside him. Perhaps the clouds hanging over his wife would soon dissipate.

————

Eric tugged his black suit coat tighter around him. An icy breeze beat against his body, seeping through the cotton fabric all the way to his bones. Winter had been harsh this year, leaving him grateful for a job that allowed him to stay indoors. That would change once summer came, though. The moment the warm air decided to stick around, he always found himself wanting out of his cramped office space in Brooklyn.

He darted up the stairs and tossed open the white door of their two-story home. The aroma that met his nose made his insides grumble. It smelled an awful lot like pie. Could Eleanor be cooking?

She'd utilized her talents in the kitchen several times over the last week, something he'd not realized he missed until their dinners had consisted of his limited experience with boxes of noodles and ready-made sauces. Even Leah had started to complain about his lack of variety.

Eric entered the kitchen and spotted a head of curly brown hair at the dining room table, just where he nearly always found her upon arriving home. Leah dipped her brush into a pool of pink paint, so focused that she didn't look up until she had created a nice blob on her white canvas.

"Hello, sweetheart," he said, bending down to kiss the top of her head. "How was school today?"

"Good." She pulled her lips to one side, and her brows pinched. "Actually, not that good. We're learning subtraction. I don't like it."

Eric suppressed a laugh. "Well, subtraction is an important skill. You'll need to know how to do it, even when you're older."

"Mrs. Wilkins said that. But I still don't *like* it."

He suspected his daughter would rather apply herself to an art class than math. He leaned over her shoulder, taking in her newest creation. The pink armor and the curly-haired knight once again graced her picture. The knight stood in a field of purple grass with a dark-gray sky looming overhead, her yellow sword held at the ready to defeat whatever villain lay in wait.

He wondered what had prompted her sudden interest in knights and swords; she'd painted several similar scenes over the last few days.

"I'm still waiting for my turn to be the knight," he said.

Leah shrugged, adding more purple grass to her picture. "You could paint your own."

Eric grimaced. He could attempt it, but his skill with a brush nearly rivaled that of using the stove and oven.

Another waft of sweet-smelling pastry grabbed his attention, and Eric slipped into the kitchen. Eleanor carried the culprit of his rumbling tummy between two oven mitts, making her way to the counter to set down a freshly baked pie —cherry, if he had to guess.

"You've been busy," said Eric, eyeing the ensemble of bowls of other scrumptious-looking food. Mashed potatoes, fruit salad, and some kind of crusted chicken all had his mouth watering. This was certainly better than the macaroni and cheese he had planned.

Eleanor swiped her hair from her face with the floral-patterned mitt and smiled. "Today was a good day. I haven't had the desire to bake in a while. I thought I might surprise you. Cherry is still your favorite, isn't it?"

His lips lifted so high they hurt. Even if it wasn't his favorite, it would be today. "Cherry pie sounds fantastic." Eric gave his wife a kiss. "What can I help you with?"

———

Eric pulled the quilted blanket over Leah's head, inciting her giggles. When she pushed it away, her smile stretched from one side of her face to the other, and her curls stuck out on all sides. He'd come home late tonight and wanted to spend a few minutes with her before she went to bed.

"How was your day?" he asked, tucking her in.

"We're doing subtraction again."

A chuckle escaped him before he could stop it. "All right, other than *that*, how was your day?"

"Good. Mommy made pork chops. They're my favorite."

He nodded, the reminder of his full plate of food yet to be eaten making his stomach complain. "Much better than Daddy's cooking, isn't it?"

She pinched her lips. "Noodles aren't so bad sometimes."

"Agreed. We should keep the noodles to just *sometimes*." He gave her a hug and a kiss before moving to the door. With the flip of the switch, darkness filled her room. "Goodnight, Leah."

"Goodnight, Daddy."

Eric returned to the kitchen, where Eleanor was busy washing dishes. "I can do those if you'd like?"

She shook her head. "You haven't even eaten yet. I'll manage."

Eric took his plate to the dining room, but before he could sit down, his gaze fell on the stack of paintings on the edge of the table. He began thumbing through Leah's pictures. Most of them displayed the knight in pink armor, but the scenes were different. They ranged from fields of purple grass to castle backdrops; one even had the brave warrior facing a gray dragon with enormous fangs.

Eleanor's light footsteps announced her presence before he even looked up. He smiled at her, holding the stack of art in front of him. "She's got a thing for knights."

"Yes, and each one of those has a story to go with it. She paints me a new one every day and then cuddles up to tell me what her brave warrior does to color the gloom."

Eric drew his brows together and tilted his head. "Color the gloom?"

She moved to his side and pointed at the gray sky on the top picture. "The gloom. Sometimes it's the sky, sometimes a dragon or some other monstrosity. The knight always uses her sword to defeat it. That's why the weapon is yellow." Eleanor nibbled at her lip, and her eyes glistened. "I think the gloom is meant to be my depression."

"What makes you think that?" Of course, Leah would have noticed the change in her mother, but did her art really reflect her observation?

Eleanor sighed and lifted one shoulder a little. "I don't know for certain, I guess. Either way, her stories have given me courage to fight. If a knight in pink armor can chase away the gloom, then I can too."

Eric dropped his gaze to the picture. "Not chase it away, but color it to something different. Something better. We may need to get you a magical yellow sword."

She giggled and rested her hand on his arm. "I already have a magical sword—two, in fact. Without them I would fail to escape my shadows."

As he watched Eleanor clear the table, Eric decided tomorrow he would take Leah up on her offer and paint his own knight. He'd told his daughter that one day her art might inspire others, but it seemed it already had. Leah had given Eleanor hope, and though the knight in pink armor wasn't likely to inspire the world, it had brought change to his small part of it.

# PHASES OF THE MOON

## ABBY FEENSTRA

Carlynne sat up straight in the back seat of the car, hands folded in her lap, looking out the window. Her big, blocky purse leaned against her legs. Her green blouse fit seamlessly into her pencil skirt. Her stiletto heels matched her outfit perfectly. Her long, silvery blonde hair was twisted into a tight chignon at the back of her head. Everything about her radiated control, flawlessness, power.

Except, of course, for the fact that her window view was obscured by the black netted bag over her head. Also, the car was driven by two men she had never met before, and she had no knowledge of their destination.

The bag was expected, of course, although that had not stopped her from giving the shorter of the men her trademark withering glare as he had approached her in the parking lot behind the Virgil bar. He had faltered, wordlessly holding out the bag. He had probably expected to pull the bag over her head himself, as he likely did with every other person he dealt with. Then again, the majority of the people he encountered in this situation were probably teenage girls, already terrified out of their wits and wracked with shame, likely to submit to anything. People her age, composed people, people with schedules and expectations and a clear path, those people did not get themselves into this sort of situation.

But that was no reason to lose her power, her control. She might be here for the same reason as those teenage girls, but that did not mean she was anything like them. She knew enough about the world to know that these men might very well be taking her not to an underground doctor but to a warehouse where she would be locked in a windowless room and eventually shipped abroad into sex slavery. Or another kind of windowless room, the kind with a two-way mirror and an FBI agent waiting for her. She didn't know which would be worse. But regardless of what was waiting for her at the end of this car ride—an exam table, a cell, an interrogation chamber—she needed to present herself as steely and powerful. Someone not to be fucked with.

The car turned, slowed, and stopped. As the driver cut the engine, Carlynne listened hard for any clues to their location. They couldn't be far from downtown, not with that short of a car ride. Maybe the edge of the suburbs? The suburbs were dangerous, full of people who had been integral to toppling the ruling, people who were the first to cheer in the streets when it finally came crashing down.

Carlynne did not remember that day herself, of course, considering that she had been a fetus at the time. But she had grown up in the Post World, and not just anywhere, but here, in Utah, where she had learned quickly what happened to outsiders. The suburbs were the last area she would expect this place to be, which may have been why they were here. Or, potentially, the suburbs were an indication that the cell, or the FBI agent, was the likelier outcome at this point.

The car door opened and Carlynne stepped out, not waiting for someone to grab her. She held out her arm, making it clear she expected somebody to take it and lead her. She was not going to be pushed along, or worse, made to step forward on her own, groping in the air before her. There was nothing that would make her look more weak, less in control.

One of the men from the parking lot, she guessed the taller one, took her arm and guided her forward. She could hear the other man walking ahead, a door opening. The ground was smooth and slightly sloped, like a driveway. The man holding her arm muttered, "Watch your step," and Carlynne ascended what could only be a set of porch stairs, confirming her suspicions. They were in the suburbs, in the heart of danger. There would be no safe place for her here, nowhere to hide. These people were her only way out.

The second she heard the front door of the house click shut behind her, the man dropped her arm. She immediately pulled the hood off her head. The two men were vanishing down a long, dim, wide hallway.

She turned to look at the door they'd just entered through —surely there was a window? The two long, floor-to-ceiling windows on either side of the door were stained glass. They were stunning, really, beautiful depictions of angels reaching up to the heavens, but completely useless. She could have seen the outline of a person standing on the porch, but she could not see enough detail of the outside world to know where they were.

She smiled. These people were the real deal. She had finally, finally found a way to solve her problem.

———

Three weeks earlier, Carlynne had needed eggs. She had to buy eggs. But she was nauseated, repulsed, standing in front of the waist-high, open refrigerator at the grocery store, staring at all the cartons of eggs. How many brands of eggs were there? What was the difference between all these eggs? Carlynne had never noticed any clear distinction between chickens, not that she spent much time around chickens, but still. It was ridiculous to have so many eggs. How could one even choose?

Of course, she grabbed the same carton she always grabbed, the expensive one, the one from a "family farm." Usually, she felt a hint of pride as she chose this carton, with its photo of the farmer and his wife and two smiling sons, over all the others in their mass-produced Styrofoam. But this time, as she popped open the lid and slowly twisted each egg, checking for viability, she once again felt mushy, hot liquid rising up in the back of her throat.

What if she threw up all over these eggs? The fifty-five different brand names and carton styles, all rendered incomprehensible, the same shade of bile green.

Thinking about throwing up made the possibility of actually throwing up seem more immediate and real. Carlynne methodically closed the egg carton, set it on top of the other groceries in her cart, and wheeled the cart around toward the front of the store. Fresh air—that was what she needed. The grocery store, with its produce and its cleaning products and its endless advertisements with photos of smiling women providing wholesome meals for their families, was the absolute last place she should be.

She felt a stab of annoyance at the people ahead of her in the checkout line, at the too-slow clerk, a woman with curly gray hair and cat-eye glasses. She was smiling and nodding at every customer, making small talk, laughing gently or rolling her eyes. Oh yes, don't I know it, if the prices keep going up I'm not going to be able to afford to eat either.

Her expression changed when she saw Carlynne. The smile

fell from her face, leaving a hard, shrewd look. Carlynne stared back, remaining silent when the woman asked how her day was going and whether she'd found everything okay. Her eyes flicked to the clerk's name tag. Sandra. What a stupid name.

Sandra was now looking down, focusing on the groceries. "Weirdly hot out there for a May day, isn't it?"

What? The weather was perfectly normal. "I don't know what you mean," Carlynne said.

Sandra looked up at Carlynne and back down. "These are unusual times, is what I'm saying."

Right. Carlynne took a deep breath. She imagined herself pushing through the checkout line, sprinting out the front doors, standing under the wide, blue, hot sky… and then where would she go? There are some things you cannot outrun.

"You know…" Sandra seemed to be ringing up Carlynne's groceries far slower than she had for the other patrons. "I hear there are steps people can take if they're trying to beat the heat."

Part of Carlynne wished she lived in Sandra's world, where apparently the biggest problem was the now-constant heat wave. Another part of Carlynne, the bigger part, wanted to reach across the register and hit Sandra right across her placid face. What did Sandra ever have to worry about? The woman was at least fifty. Carlynne cleared her throat and looked at her watch.

"Of course," Sandra chuckled and looked straight at Carlynne. "It's a little hard for us to stay cool here in the store when they give us these ridiculous double-ply uniform shirts." She grabbed the bottom of her shirt and waved it in and out to fan herself.

Carlynne was about to slam her hand on the register, to say she was in a hurry, she didn't want to talk about the weather anymore, she might actually kill Sandra if the woman didn't start ringing up her damn groceries—and then she saw it. A tiny tattoo, a small series of dots on Sandra's bare hip, only visible for the minutest of instants. Dots that started small and gradually morphed into crescents, and then half circles, and then a single full circle that tapered back down to nothing.

The phases of the moon.

Carlynne was suddenly aware of how much space Sandra had created between Carlynne and the next customer, a large, beefy man. She took a deep breath. "Well, I'm sorry I can't do anything about those shirts. But I would love to hear more about those other… tips… you had suggested. To stay cool."

Sandra smiled and grabbed the next item on the belt, a box of crackers. "Well, the main thing I keep hearing is just to stay calm. I know that sounds pretty basic and like it wouldn't make much of a difference, but you know, the heat can really mess with your emotions, make things seem worse than they are. You hear about people making rash decisions sometimes, you know." Carlynne's stomach twisted and fluttered. Maybe she had made a mistake. Maybe she had misread the situation.

Sandra continued. "And you know the other thing I hear?" She laughed and shook her head. "This one's going to sound even more ridiculous, I bet, but I guess it's true: the stuff you eat can make a big difference. Supposedly, your body is a lot better at cooling you down if you eat a lot of non-meat protein." She lifted up the carton of eggs and winked at Carlynne. "Like these."

They had come to the end of Carlynne's groceries. The beefy man was now standing just a few feet behind her, tapping his foot.

Carlynne smiled the kind of indulgent smile a younger woman gives an older one dispensing absurd life advice. "You know what, I might try that. Thanks."

Sandra slid the eggs into the last grocery bag and handed it to Carlynne. "You're welcome, honey. You have a good day now."

When Carlynne was home, she waited for her hands to stop shaking before pulling the egg carton out of the bag. Inside, tucked under one of the eggs, was a small piece of receipt paper, ripped from the roll on one edge and folded into eighths. "Virgil Bar, downtown. Three weeks. Back parking lot. Wear green."

————

"Okay." The doctor exhaled and pushed her stool backward. "You're all good. You can sit up, but do it slowly."

Carlynne exhaled too, not moving yet. Her head swam. She was not in pain, physical or emotional, contrary to the popular narrative. But she was drained. All that work, all those weeks, all the uncertainty, and the act itself had taken less than fifteen minutes.

She sat up, slowly, and looked around her. It was hard to imagine a room more ridiculous for a medical procedure. It was barely wide enough for the exam table, which was not so much an exam table as it was a kitchen table on which a thin cot had been placed and under which the doctor stored her tools in a plastic carton. The "room" itself was hidden behind a fake wall in the basement of the doctor's house.

Everything was perfectly sanitary and safe, the doctor had assured her. She shouldn't worry about the stirrups screwed to the table's edge—they had been personally designed and built by an engineer. The wax paper sheet covering the cot, the latex gloves the doctor was now yanking off, the thin gown she was wearing, those were all the exact same brands she would encounter in a hospital. All the sanitation procedures were up to medical industry standards. The doctor had apologized extensively for the components that were not "right": the room, the house, the hood, the car ride, the secrecy. "We try to make this whole thing as dignified as possible," she had said, "because that's really what our movement is about—the preservation of dignity, the dignity that's been taken away from all women. But obviously, we've had to make some concessions."

It had been ironic to talk of dignity with a woman whose face she could not see—although that, of course, was one of the concessions. Carlynne had not expected anything less. The doctor could be killed by firing squad for what she was doing. Carlynne did find the choice of face obscurement questionable, though. Above the doctor's blue surgical mask, an ornate, green-and-gold cat mask hid the rest of her face. The seven phases of the moon, the same symbol that had brought Carlynne here, swirled in a semi-circle around the mask's left eye.

Below the neck, however, the woman looked just like any other doctor, albeit one whose white medical coat was missing a name tag. Gloves now removed, the doctor made a few notes on her tablet before turning back to Carlynne. "So. Some things to keep in—"

"Excuse me." Damn it. Her voice had cracked. Carlynne cleared her throat and tried again. "May I ask what, exactly, is the information you're recording on there?" She lifted a finger to indicate the tablet.

"Of course." The doctor nodded smoothly, the cat mask flashing in the fluorescent ceiling light. "We record details of the procedure as part of research into improving future care. There's no longer funding or facilities for this particular area of health care, unfortunately, so we can't let the data go to waste. We do record some of your personal information as part of our data collection—not your name, obviously, but your age, your ethnicity, any relevant preexisting conditions, how many weeks. You can be assured this data is securely encrypted and stored on a server located outside of the country. And also, the sheer amount of women we serve will afford each individual woman a significant measure of protection and anonymity in the unlikely event of a breach." The doctor smiled wanly. "Safety in numbers."

"What about your protection?" A part of Carlynne was still struggling with disbelief. To be a woman in a professional setting was rare enough in these times; she had assumed her doctor would be male. To be a woman and to choose such a risk...

The doctor barked a brief, humorless laugh. "That should be your ultimate assurance that we do everything in our power to protect this data. There are thousands of people like you, but very few like me. Were I to lose track of this information, the government would be at my door in a matter of moments." She shook her head. "Now, for you. Like I said, you're lucky enough to still have been pretty early, so it wasn't the most intense procedure, but you should still expect some soreness and bleeding. I would wear a maxi pad for the next few days if I were you."

"Will I need any medication?"

"You should be fine with over-the-counter stuff. Most women report—" She stopped. No woman reported anything anymore.

There was a brief pause.

"The literature shows that the most pain the majority of patients experience is similar to and no worse than regular menstrual cramps." She folded her hands in her lap. "Any other questions?"

"Yes." Carlynne looked the other woman straight in the

eye. "What should I expect in the future from your organization?"

The doctor nodded. "Continued surveillance," she said
matter-of-factly. "For both your safety and ours. Complications
are rare, not nearly as common as the propaganda makes them
out to be, but they can happen, so you will be monitored
closely for about the next week. Your phone will continue
backing up to our cloud for an unspecified length of time,
usually between three and five years, and then the link will be
terminated if we don't see anything concerning. Based on your
age and assets, you'll probably be taken off our watchlist
sooner rather than later. Our biggest liability is the younger
ones, especially the teenagers. The feds are a lot more likely to
keep an eye on them, and they get scared pretty easily." The
doctor's eyes flicked towards Carlynne. The effect was unnerv-
ing, under the cat's face. "You don't seem to be someone who's
scared of much, though."

"I'm not," Carlynne said shortly. She stood up, her legs
between the table's silver stirrups, and looked pointedly at
the pile of her clothing, folded neatly and stacked at the
table's head. It was time for her to leave this place and
move on.

The doctor obligingly slid her stool backward, giving
Carlynne room to move to the top of the cot. "You know," she
said as she stood up, "we don't get a lot of women in here like
you."

Carlynne flushed. As if she needed a reminder.

"But there are a lot of women like you out there." The
doctor tipped her head to the side, studying Carlynne frankly.
"Professional women. Women without a lot of connections to
other women. It's ironic that women with the most financial
resources and career independence these days are often the
ones most likely to be boxed into a corner, the least likely to

find us, or anyone who knows about us." The doctor paused. "May I ask how you knew?"

Carlynne stared at the doctor. "My aunt," she said finally. "She was big in the anti-ruling protest movement back in the day. She kept it up, even a decade after The Overturning. My dad…" Carlynne pushed her shoulders back. "When she went to prison, my dad said she'd had it coming. But I remember those last few years…" She pointed to the moons, twining around the doctor's eye. "She had moons everywhere. Her clothes, her jewelry, she even doodled them all over the birthday cards she'd send me. Looking back, it was obvious she was trying to show me a path out, if I ever needed it." She shook her head. "I guess she knew that one day I would."

"We all do." The doctor's eyes remained on Carlynne's face. "Some people need different paths. And one day, hopefully, there will be a clear path for every one of us again. There are more of us than there are of them, although it doesn't feel that way. And there are quite a few of us who are just like you."

The two women, the doctor in the cat mask and the lawyer in the hospital gown, were quiet, facing each other.

"My aunt always said I had pretty ears," Carlynne said finally. "She would give me earrings often, as Christmas and birthday gifts."

It was hard to tell, but Carlynne thought she could see a spark in the doctor's cat eyes. "Your aunt sounds like she had very, very good taste."

———

Anita took deep breaths, in through her nose and out through her mouth, as she walked steadily down the corridor to the elevator. It didn't matter what was going on in one's personal life, a judge—particularly a female judge—could not let it spill over into the courtroom. In the ten years since Anita had ascended to the bench, she had gotten used to the sharp intakes of breath from the gallery when she entered court. Of course, the number of judges who looked like her had only dwindled during that decade. And she had heard the whispers, three years ago, when she had dared to come back from her maternity leave.

As the elevator doors closed behind her, Anita shut her eyes. That was just it, wasn't it? It was already outlandish enough that she was in this position as a woman, a Latina, a mother. What would happen when people found out and she had to go through it all again? To say nothing of how they would afford it, with childcare cost what it was. Plus, she was still getting medical bills from all the complications from the twins.

She could hear her mother's voice: *That's what you get for waiting so long.* Well, the joke was on Anita now. She had prayed so hard in her late thirties, knowing she would need all the help she could get. God must have thought she would take this new development as a blessing, a surprise bonus.

The elevator stopped on the sixth floor, and a tall woman with long, silvery-blonde hair stepped in. Anita recognized her: Carlynne Barrett, one of the few female lawyers who regularly cycled through Anita's court. Anita respected Carlynne— she respected any woman who had made partner, and she knew Carlynne was ambitious enough to maybe be eyeing a judgeship one day. But she could not have a mentorship conversation right now. She simply could not. Especially not with a woman a few years younger than her, a woman who wore no wedding ring, who had clearly made her choices and would never find herself in the same stupid situation as Anita.

Luckily, mentorship and networking did not seem to be on

Carlynne's mind. She smiled briefly at Anita before stabbing the lobby button and turning to face the door.

"It's absurdly hot out, isn't it?" Carlynne glanced at Anita. When the other woman made no response, she went on. "It really makes me miss the beginning of summer. What I wouldn't give for a nice, cool May day, you know?"

May day?

Anita's heart skipped a beat. It had to be a coincidence. She watched Carlynne out of the corner of her eye, but the woman stared placidly ahead, sipping out of her coffee cup.

Ding. They had reached the lobby. Carlynne smiled at Anita. "Well, have a good day, Your Honor."

She stepped forward and the coffee cup left her hand. Anita yelled and sprang back as the cup landed at her feet, sending scalding liquid all over the hem of her robe. She glared at Carlynne, suddenly furious. She imagined cracking the other woman across the face with the files in her hand, the gasps of the onlookers in the lobby, the whispers—you know what they say about mothers who try to still have a career, looks like Judge Gonzalez is finally falling apart under the pressure...

"I am so sorry." Carlynne immediately pulled a pile of napkins out of her purse and, businesslike, swept her long hair over one shoulder and knelt at Anita's feet to sop up the liquid.

"Counselor." Anita's breathing was shallow. "I have to tell you, today of all—"

She froze. Looking down at Carlynne, her hair over her left shoulder and her right ear exposed, she could just barely see it. Tattooed dots on the back of Carlynne's ear, each dot slowly growing in size then receding, the largest no bigger than the head of a pin.

The phases of the moon.

# YELLOW CROCUS

## BRADLEY S. BLANCHARD

T he prison tower isn't so bad. It's quite lovely actually, when you consider execution as the alternative.

It was a chilly spring day, but the square below was already alive with activity. A soft light was just creeping over the square, setting the yellow avens aglow. They were beautiful, and I was running out of yellow ochre paint.

I smoothed my worn blue dress and considered my situation as I painted. The King's choice was simple, really. If the baby was his, I had slandered His Queen, and by extension, the entire kingdom, and the penalty for me was death. If the baby wasn't his, I had spoken the truth, and the Queen had attempted to cuckold the King, and the penalty for the Queen, and the baby, was death. If it was anyone else's baby, I wouldn't care, but it wasn't just anyone else's baby, it was Dag's baby. I was sure of it.

My choice wasn't much better. Wait several weeks for more yellow ochre to arrive or try using yellow crocus instead. I never seemed to get the shading right with paint made from yellow crocus.

All morning I waited for the church bells to peal in celebration. Antsy. Painting. Pacing. Sketching. Waiting. Alternating between excitement and disappointment. If they rang out, the child was the royal heir. If they didn't, there was no royal heir.

By noon it was decided. No bells meant I won. There were no bells, so I had won.

If I won, his baby lost.

Not for the first time, anger rose in me. Dag always made everything complicated. I loved him. I hated him. I wanted him back. I wanted his memory to just leave me alone. And he'd died just like he had lived, leaving a mess of everything he had touched.

My jailer outside my door spoke to his replacement. "Was the babe born?"

"Two months early but fat as a suckling pig. Shock of golden hair."

"King don't have no straw color hair," said the first.

Neither did the Queen.

"She tried to cuckold him for sure," said his replacement. "He's got the old men checking the descent lines for any mention of gold hair, blue eyes, but I'm thinking Queen and baby…" There was a *schwit* sound, like someone drawing a knife across a throat.

"Shame. We could use a royal bawler to secure the line and all."

"If the King ain't got no arrows in his quiver, when he dies, there will be war for sure."

Looks like I had secured my freedom, and all it had cost was an innocent child, a not so innocent queen, and the hopes of an entire kingdom.

———

The story, of course, started months ago. I had arrived from Estate Cederberg to attend court. I was wearing my best dress, a worn blue item with fraying cuffs and a dirty hem. The rest of the court was dressed in red velvets and white silks. Rubies and diamonds were on display around their throats, on their fingers, sewn into clothing. I had no jewels: my grandparents had sold them decades before.

The room, as always, smelled of roses and perfumes with an undercurrent of human body odor.

Truth, I looked more like a servant than a noble. As the lowest ranking and poorest noble in the kingdom, I was tolerated but not really included, like an annoying little sister who tags along after an older one. I listened to the gossip but had nothing to add.

*The war might be coming to an end.*

*The Queen had been sick this morning.*

*A new ambassador might be appointed soon. She was considering a commoner.*

That last caught my attention. Panic had flooded me. The last two royal playthings who got appointed ambassadors had ended up dead. Dag, my former betrothed, was the current royal plaything. Before I could inquire for more information, a perfectly pitched tenor cut me off, announcing the Queen.

Court went… poorly. Queen Tania had a glow to her face that I'd never seen before. Her black hair seemed even more lustrous. Her red silk and velvet dress, set off by the diamond choker around her neck, made her even more enthralling. I hated her for it.

"You may attend," she said, seating herself on her throne. The dais had five steps. His Majesty's throne was at the top; hers sat one step down.

"Estate reports," she commanded. "Smallest first."

By smallest she meant poorest, and that meant me.

Before she stole Dag from me for her bed, she had been indifferent toward me. Now, every week for the last five months, estate reports started with me.

I approached the throne, reminding myself that despite my family's current fortunes, I belonged here. Stopping short of the first step, I looked up. Queen Tania smelled of lavender, roses, and bliss.

"Estate Cederberg is the same as last report."

"Still falling down?" she said, her voice light, playful. There were titters behind me. I felt my face go red.

Truth. It was falling down. I had a patron who gave me enough to eat and to paint but not enough to fix anything.

"Perhaps we should take up a collection?"

"No need, Your Majesty," I said.

She arched an eyebrow. You weren't supposed to disagree with either of their Royal Majesties.

"Perhaps less time in court and more time making money." The Queen waved me away. It was not a return to your peers gesture. It was a leave court gesture.

My face flushed. I held my head high and made a stately retreat from the room. As I was going out, I passed Commander Aelin coming in. She had a scalp with several scars. All healed. Her clothes were clean of blood. Her face was intense but calm, not grim. Good news about the war then. We could use some good news.

I strolled down the hall of portraits. Kings and Queens back to the founding of the kingdom, Taiga. Brown and black hair. Brown and green eyes. None like Dag, with his piercing blue eyes and golden blond hair.

I didn't look for signatures. I could name all the court painters by the style of their strokes. The style of Bergen's Queen Yaffa was closest to my own. Queen Yaffa wasn't a blonde, but she looked like the person who would want to be one.

———

Before heading home, I went to see Waiola, the royal apothecary. I was working on a painting of Dag and had run out of yellow ochre. I was always running out of yellow ochre. In a pinch, I used yellow crocus, even though I could never get the shading right with yellow crocus.

"My lady," Waiola said as I entered. Cut, dried flowers hung from the walls. The hut smelled of spices, laudanum, mint, and pig feces.

"I need yellow crocus," I said.

She nodded. "Take what you need, but don't take it all."

Out back, as I sorted through the piles of dried and drying plants, I could hear Waiola talking to her apprentice.

"The war is over and the King returns on the morrow? Well, she'll be wanting a Royal Cure today. Best see how much pennyroyal we have left. We'll have to hope it's enough. Oh, and acacia, for when the King returns. Kingdom needs an heir, and they'll need all the help they can get."

Acacia was for male infertility, which His Majesty would never admit to. But why pennyroyal?

I ran through its uses. Rheumatism, which the Queen didn't have.

Smallpox. No.

Body lice? I could only hope.

Abortifacient? I thought of her glowing face and lustrous hair. My chest clamped up, and my breath wheezed in and out of my chest. The world seemed to spin around me.

Pennyroyal was most effective early in pregnancy. His Majesty was coming home. Our Queen apparently didn't want to be caught pregnant with someone else's child. She was only sleeping with one person I knew of.

Who else suspected? Not the court or the servants, or rumors of the pregnancy would race throughout the kingdom. Waiola and her apprentice? Probably. So, three of us, but those two would never share.

Queen Tania had made her two previous lovers ambassadors and had them killed on the way to their postings. One by bandits. The other by poisoning.

Court rumor mentioned a commoner being considered for ambassador. I grabbed the edge of the drying rack as my legs threatened to fail me.

Dag.

She would kill him, just like the previous two ambassadors. Then abort the baby. Gossip would be the only evidence of her trysts. That and the paintings stashed in my attic.

What Queen Tania wanted, I opposed on principle. And because I loved Dag. Also, because I didn't like her.

I reached past the dried flowers for the freshly cut pennyroyal, recognizable by the purple flowers and smell of mint.

"My lady," said Waiola, coming around the corner. "Yellow crocus would be yellow, not purple."

I gave her a tight smile. "Just so."

Gathering up an armful of yellow crocus, I hurried past her, head still spinning.

So maybe I couldn't save the baby, but I could still save Dag.

———

I was unsaddling Elis when I found the note. The stable was designed for sixteen horses but hadn't regularly held over two at a time in the last half century. It, like the house, was too big and falling into disrepair.

Opening the note, I immediately recognized Dag's writing.

*Come away with me. I leave this afternoon.*

My heart fluttered in my chest. I realized I was bouncing on my toes. To have him back. I sighed a sigh of contentment in the cool shadows. Elis snorted. Even the horse knew it was a bad idea.

Rushing into the house, with its worn wooden floors and leaky roof, I felt a pang of guilt at leaving.

I loved Cederberg. I loved Kingdom Taiga. But I loved Dag most.

I hurried to gather my things, which weren't much. Three well-used dresses. A hairbrush my grandmother gave me. Food from the kitchen, but no dishes. I passed the painting room, which faced east to get the morning light. My eyes flicked past my paintings to the piece of the ceiling where I had hidden two paintings.

I had done both of them from other sketches.

The first painting was Queen Tania with Lord Sjodin. He was splayed out on the royal bed, half dressed, ambassador commission in his hand. He was her first plaything after His Majesty went to war.

The second was of His Grace, Duke Sund, lying on the ground, sword through his chest, ambassador commission in hand. The emblem of the Queen's Guard, a red ruby surrounded by five coins, was on the chest of the man killing Duke Sund. Her second plaything.

I had painted them, thinking I would give them to His Majesty and get Queen Tania in trouble, then decided they would likely just land me in prison instead. And so they had.

His Majesty might overlook a royal tryst, especially in his

absence. Murder of a noble was more serious, but I couldn't prove it… yet.

There was a knock at the kitchen door in the back. I rushed to it and found Dag waiting. Boyish good looks. Golden yellow hair. Piercing blue eyes.

He picked me up and swung me around. I laughed, my heart leaping. I'd been miserable since Queen Tania had stolen him from me almost half a year ago.

He set me down as we looked at one other expectantly. The silence drew us close. He smelled of lavender and roses, just like the Queen. The silence became uncomfortable. I tried to ignore both the silence and the smell.

"Her Majesty wishes to make me ambassador to Adad-Shammura."

My heart sank. Dag could not refuse a royal request any more than I could. His Majesty considered a refusal to be treason against the kingdom.

Gravel crunched underfoot as, bag in hand, I headed to the stable. Dag followed.

"But we're not going to Adad-Shammura. Right?" I hated the way my words were anxious, almost pleading.

He raced in front of me, stopping in the doorway to the stables. The smell of hay and horse manure drifted past him. The day was warm, the sun bright. His hair was golden in the sunlight. His eyes were a piercing blue.

"No. We're going to go wherever you want." His voice was full of smiles and promises.

I stepped in close. Again that smell. Roses and lavender. Had he just come from the Queen?

My face flushed. My body trembled with anticipation. I wanted to go. I wanted to cry. I wanted to be left alone. I wanted to stare into those blue eyes forever.

Dag was my heart and soul, but I knew his love would fade the moment he found someone with more prestige, more power, more wealth, more beauty. It was like cold water to the face.

I wasn't sure if Queen Tania was his true love either. Is it wrong to say I hoped he was using her, just like she was using him?

"What?" he said, sensing something had changed.

I would go with him, but only long enough to make sure he was safe.

"Nothing," I said, but we both knew it was a lie.

"Someone's here," Dag said, standing in the doorway. His horse was all ready to travel. I was still cinching up Elis' saddle.

"Quick. In here." I waved him in. "You can hide in the stable until they're gone."

Dag grabbed his horse and rushed to the far end of the stable. Before I could call him closer, the pounding of hooves accosted my ears. Six riders approached, all bearing the emblem of five gold coins surrounding a red ruby. Voss, Captain of the Queen's Guard, slid off his big, black stallion. His face was the same as the one in the painting. A chill crept down my spine.

"My lady," Voss said. "Have you seen Mister Dag?"

"Who?" I asked, trying to look wide-eyed and oblivious. Dag's horse took that moment to neigh, and my horse knickered.

We could try to outrun them, but they said Voss had the fastest horse in the kingdom. We wouldn't get far if we ran.

Voss pushed past me and into the stable. He looked at both horses. One in the stall closest to the door, the other at the far end of the stable. Both ready to travel. He frowned, considered, and then quickly rapped twice on a stall.

Dag's head popped up from the far end of the stable. I love Dag, but he's dense at times.

Voss smiled, pushed his dark brown hair out of his eyes, and held out a paper.

"Mister Dag, your commission."

———

It's my fault Dag died on the way to Adad-Shammura. The eight of us were several weeks into the journey and getting ready to spend our first night crossing The Black Fens. There was no reason for it, other than our leader, Captain Voss of the Queen's Guard, said it would be safer. Fewer bandits.

Fewer bandits but more mosquitos and biting flies. Higher chance of Black Fen Fever.

The Queen's Guard was more loyal than smart and more tough than creative. No bandits hid in the fens. That meant they would likely try to poison us or have something venomous do the job.

As we got ready to enter The Black Fens, our escort pulled out a bag of green powder.

"What does that do?" I asked.

"Keeps away bugs and flies," said Voss.

He passed me the bag. I sniffed it. I didn't trust it. I passed it back.

Dag took the bag when they were done and covered himself. I sidled up to Dag.

"Don't use it," I whispered. "Possibly poison."

Dag laughed. "Why would they poison themselves?" he whispered back.

The day was long and wet. By the time we camped for the night, all I wanted to do was eat and get some sleep. The cook gave us our food first. I took Dag's plate over to him and sat down but fell asleep before I could eat anything.

When I woke up the next morning, I saw my plate was gone but thought little of it. Coming back to camp, after some needed relief, I could see Voss already saddling his big black stallion.

"Morning."

He looked at me like he'd seen a ghost then shook his head clear and said, "Morning, Lady Cederberg." I could feel his eyes on me as I moved back into camp.

Walking up to Dag, I bent down and shook him and called his name softly. "Dag."

No response. I tried again. That's when I noticed his skin was waxy, yellow, like he'd had Black Fen Fever. He wasn't breathing. I pulled back an eyelid. Dag's eyes had rolled up into the back of his head. Black Fen Fever didn't do that.

I screamed. Five Queen's Guards, in various states of undress, rushed over, weapons drawn. Voss and the cook exchanged a look. A sixth guard didn't move. I ran over to him, and one glance told me his skin was waxy and yellow. My empty food tray lay near him. I didn't bother to check his eyes. He had been poisoned, just like Dag.

Voss drew his sword and strode towards me. I turned and almost bumped into his horse. Mounting it, I gave a kick and galloped out of camp, leaving them with the other unsaddled horses to stare after me.

Truth. Voss really had the fastest horse in the kingdom. He also had a note in his saddlebag:

*Take them through The Black Fens.*

Someone had drawn a small map showing a spot with a pit with snakes.

The note was unsigned, but I had a pretty good guess who it belonged to.

———

My return was stressful, but I made it back before Voss. The kingdom was flooded with news that the Queen was pregnant with a royal heir. It was a miracle, they said, a reward for a righteous king. He was gone, came back, and boom. A baby was coming.

I stopped by Estate Cederberg to get two of my paintings on my way to the palace. It was a court day, after all.

When I showed up in court, no one was more surprised than Queen Tania. Her eyes widened, and her mouth made silent sounds.

I strode past the other nobles in their red silks and velvets, aware of my dirty blue dress with its mud and dirt stains, two paintings tucked under my arm. A low murmur washed through the room. The noble at the foot of the dais, Lady Sunderberg, took one look at me and stepped out of the way.

I walked right up to the dais, head held high, and stared at Queen Tania until she looked back. She still had that glow, and one hand rested idly on her stomach.

"Royal Cure didn't take, Your Majesty?" I said, looking my queen in the eye, not waiting to be given permission to speak.

"Lady…" The King tapped his fingers on his throne, looking down on me from his perch, "… Cederberg. How come you to us looking like…" He gestured with his hands to encompass the mud, dirt, and general disorder of my demeanor. "And full of such disrespect."

"Your Majesty, I was most recently accompanying the newest ambassador, Dag Dulain, to his duty post in Adad-Shamurra—"

"We know he's dead," cut in the Queen. "That you poisoned him and stole Captain Voss' horse." She reached her right hand up and put it on His Majesty's left forearm.

"No, my Queen." I said the last through gritted teeth. "He was murdered. Killed by the Queen's Guard, like the two other ambassadors that shared your bed. And I took that horse to save my life."

"Silence," His Majesty roared, placing his left hand on the Queen's right. "You may not slander our kingdom thus. Prove your charges or face beheading for sedition."

I pulled out the first painting.

"The man in the royal bed with the queen is Lord Sund."

"Send for him," said His Majesty, looking down on the assembled crowd like an angry god.

"He's abroad," said the Queen.

"You mean he's dead," I corrected. I held up the second painting. "So is His Grace, Duke Sjodin."

His Majesty's eyes narrowed. "How?"

"They were abroad," the Queen said, looking up at him with wide, loving eyes.

"Commissioned ambassadors," I added. "They never made it to their posts—"

"The roads can be dangerous," she shot back. I spoke over her.

"There was no reason to notify you because she knew they would never arrive. Not Lord Sund. Not Duke Sjodin. Not golden-haired, blue-eyed commoner, Dag Dulain."

Queen Tania had been in charge of domestic affairs while His Majesty was away at war. But he was still the sovereign and was supposed to be notified of any appointments. From the way his brows knit together, I knew she hadn't notified him.

I pulled out the note. The Queen eyed it and snatched for it when I held it up, but Commander Aelin was faster. She passed it to the King.

"The handwriting belongs to Her Majesty," I said. "I'm sure

you'll want to make a comparison." I held up a bag of green powder. "This, along with something the cook put in the meal, combines to mimic Black Fen Fever. If a greedy Queen's Guard hadn't eaten my food when I wasn't looking, I would be as dead as Dag Dulain."

There was a murmur from the assembled nobles behind me. I felt people move up behind me and expected the guards to grab me and drag me away. It was not the guards but the elderly parents of Lord Sund and the well-fed mother of Duke Sjodin.

His Majesty looked troubled.

Plotting the death of a noble was not a charge easy to sink to the bottom of the river, letting time wash it away. Beheading me over this accusation might put the nobles into revolt. Letting my slander go unchallenged risked disrespect to the throne.

"Three nobles dead and an attempt on another?" he said, his voice searching for truth.

"Two," the Queen said. "Dag Dulain was common born."

This didn't seem to make His Majesty rest any easier.

"For now, Lady Cederberg, you are to be our guest in the tower."

The prison tower.

"Yes, Your Majesty." I looked up into his face and then verbally stabbed him in the one place I knew he was vulnerable, putting him in an impossible position. "And congratulations."

He was impotent. Dag had proved that. But His Majesty had returned close enough to the baby's conception that he must have questions about whether it might be his.

"On putting you in the tower?" he said.

"On the baby. I'm sure he'll look just like his father."

Which brings us back to today.

Now I regret my last remark to His Majesty. It's not the baby's fault his mother is a horrible person. After mourning Dag for a few months, I can see he's also not the perfect person I wanted him to be.

Neither was Voss. As soon as he returned, the King had him hanged.

*Click.*

A key turned in the lock, and I turned around to face it. Excitement flooded through me. No bells meant I was free.

Commander Aelin of the King's Guard stood in the doorway, a crown encircling the sun on her chest.

"The Queen wants to see you."

"What if I don't want to see her?"

She didn't dignify that with a remark. I nodded and followed her.

I still loved Dag and still hated him for dying. I still longed to be near him and still wanted his memory to leave me alone.

We passed through the hall of portraits on our way to see the Queen. My eyes searched out Queen Yaffa as we passed. Her brown hair was lighter at the top, but I couldn't tell if Bergen had been trying to mimic the light. I tried to stop, but Commander Aelin pulled me along.

I shoved down the guilt. No bells meant I had won.

Queen Tania was in her bedchamber when I arrived with the new... prince? Bastard? I wasn't sure what to call it.

She dismissed her ladies-in-waiting and motioned me to a stool. Her black hair wasn't lustrous right now, just dull and knotted. She pointed to the cradle next to her where a perfect little baby with a shock of golden hair was sleeping.

I bent over. The baby looked at me. I could already see

Dag's boyish good looks and sun-blond hair. He was Dag in miniature, and when the baby opened his eyes, they pierced my heart.

"I'm going to be executed," the Queen said. "And the baby with me."

"Better you than me." I was still gazing at the baby, unable to look away. I didn't want to die.

Her eyes narrowed. "I'm tired of this game. Why do you hate me? I am your Queen."

The blue eyes closed, breaking their hold over me.

"You stole the man I loved." I would have done anything for the man I loved.

"But he didn't love you or he wouldn't have left," she said, then sighed. "What he wanted was your brains and my body, position, power, and wealth."

My head snapped back like she had slapped me. I toppled off the stool, landing with a thump. What she said stung my soul because it was true. Well, mostly true. Not the body part, but all the rest.

Then, I laughed. Queen Tania looked at me, splayed out on the floor, and laughed as well. And, for the moment, all the pettiness and pain drained away.

I righted the stool. "We were unfortunate enough to both love a man who wanted the best parts of each of us but was unwilling to accept all of us."

"When I came here from the Merchant Federation, I had dreams of what it would be like to be a Queen." She picked at her blanket. "I thought it would be more like a feast day and less like running a shop. I was wrong."

"If you loved Dag, why did you try to kill him? And the others?"

"Sund and Sjodin were mistakes. They weren't supposed to die. Things just happen on the road. At least, that's what Voss told me, but he lied about enough things that I wonder if he lied about that as well. Dag wasn't supposed to die." Her eyes studied the blanket, unable to meet mine. "Just you. I couldn't bear the thought of someone else having him, even though I knew from the beginning I couldn't keep him."

I didn't forgive her, but I understood her desire to keep him close. My eyes strayed to the baby.

I didn't want to die.

I could save the baby.

"Is there a way to save the baby?" she asked, genuinely worried.

I would die if I saved the baby.

"I'm sorry, Your Majesty," I said and left.

———

All night I tossed and turned, dreaming of Dag with waxy, yellow skin, eyes rolled up into the back of his head. Of a crying baby being shoved into a sack, tied to a rope, and dropped into a lake. Of walking down an endless hall of portraits.

At first light, I washed in the small basin, put on my worn blue dress, and waited for Commander Aelin to escort me to the throne room for my exoneration and the Queen's sentencing.

As we hurried down the hall of portraits, towards the throne room, we passed by Queen Yaffa.

"Fine," I shouted at the portrait.

I would die if it meant saving Dag's baby.

Commander Aelin gave me a weird look.

"Help me take this down," I said, pointing to Queen Yaffa.

"No," she said.

"No?" I poked her in the chest with my finger. She took a

step back. "Not no. Now! If you love His Majesty, you'll help me. Now."

A terrified look flashed across her face. I wondered just how close she and the King had gotten during the war. Royal prerogative?

I grabbed the portrait and ran. She was hot on my heels.

I turned the corner of the throne room just as she threw her weight at me. I lost the painting. It slid down the aisle, landing with a thunk at the base of the dais.

Commander Aelin looked like her life was a vase that had just shattered on a marble floor.

I stood and walked into the throne room.

"Your Majesty, proof that blonde hair runs in your family." I picked up the painting and handed it up to him.

"She has brown hair," he said. He wanted to believe, but he needed something credible, no matter how flimsy.

"Look closer. The roots are blonde. Queen Yaffa colored her hair."

He looked, and a smile grew across his face. "The heir is legitimate!"

A cheer went up from the assembled nobles. Queen Tania looked at me, smiled, and gave me a nod. A shock of golden hair pushed out from the baby in the blanket at her chest.

———

His Majesty commuted my sentence. Her Majesty granted Estate Cederberg a stipend, in perpetuity, that was enough to live off of and fix some things. The nobles got me named Court Painter. Truth. Queen Yaffa wasn't really a blonde. Bergen, who did her portrait, seemed to have had just as much trouble getting the shading right with yellow crocus as I did.

# OF NEEDLES AND SONGS

## J.E. ZARNOFSKY

T he executioner thrust Estella's head onto the chopping block. The slick steel halberd glistened in the high noon sun. The red syrup of blood, heavy with a rotten metallic odor, licked her cheek from the stained wooden stump. The five other so-called criminals murdered before her now stained her flesh.

Estella no longer wondered how she got there. No, those thoughts had been wasted on the weeks, or months, hidden away in the prison cell beneath the castle's walls. Instead, she mused how the miserable man with the miserable job of taking so many miserable lives could bear to wear nothing but black in the horrible humid heat of the sweltering summer sun.

From atop the dais, Duke Iren glared down at Estella as if she were feces he couldn't scrape off his servant-polished boots quickly enough. He nodded to the executioner, cleared his throat, and scanned the scroll unfurled in his hands. "Estella Minerva Ronds, I hereby sentence you to death for inciting riots within…"

"Inciting a riot, my ass. You lot did that yourselves. I was doing my damn job." She winced as the guard pressed her cheek further into the slop of blood.

The duke took a deep breath, closing his eyes and rubbing his forehead. "... within the establishment of The Sleeping Dragon Inn, and..."

Estella spit the blood from her mouth, not paying mind if it was hers. "Even in Whitemoor, winding tunes on a hurdy-gurdy while singing a few naughty verses is not a crime."

The duke's face reddened, camouflaging his fury with the red banners flying behind him. He spit at the small, helpless bard, his hands trembling. "When they are about me, they are."

She wished there was any worth in plotting an escape, but Estella could only think of all the things she wanted to say. First and foremost, she never directly called out the duke in any of her songs. If he saw himself in her woven words, that was indicative of his own insecurities and not her performances.

She opened her mouth to say just that.

She never had the chance.

The courtyard rattled. The air filled with smoke. Estella's world vanished to black.

———

Lyra gazed down at the courtyard below from the window of the former duchess's room. She gripped a needle in one wrinkled hand and her embroidery in the other. Her knuckles turned as white as her hair as if her life and the life of the woman being executed depended on never letting them go. Her breath caught as the sun glinted off of the executioner's blade, blinding her for just a moment.

A concussive force rattled the windows. The building shook.

She crumpled to the floor, the needle finding purchase in her flesh. With a yelp and a curse, she pushed to her feet, pulled the needle from her hand, and pressed her face against the window. Nothing but the smoke filled the space below as dust drifted around her. Lyra turned her head, scanning the room. She smiled in the comfort of her isolation.

The chorus of screams reached her window. The bomb had exploded according to plan, and the frenzied crowd slid into chaos. Lyra waited for the smoke to clear to see if all of her work had been worth it.

Nothing should have been damaged. Well, nothing save the textiles of everyone packed into the courtyard. The haze dissipated, and splotches emerged of the bright-orange clay dye she dropped in the street where the dissidents could retrieve it while disposing of the old duchess's belongings. In a week or two, the rains would wash the stone as if the entire incident never happened, but the blow to Duke Iren's ego, his favorite wig and finest silks stained his least favorite color, would be felt for decades to come.

The bard was nowhere to be seen.

The crowd scattered like rabbits before the wolves.

A poor facsimile of Duke Iren's head, drawn on a rotting pumpkin and complete with the lopsided white powder, orange-stained wig, rolled towards the platform and thumped against it. The executioner knelt down, unfazed by the commotion, and retrieved the rotting gourd. He returned to his post, tossing the head atop the basket of now former criminals and grabbing his halberd.

Lyra held her breath to keep herself from laughing as a tear fell from her eye. She limped across the room and returned to her work.

The hooded man's voice bellowed through the empty courtyard. "Next."

―――――

Estella awoke in a comfortable bed in a modest cottage she didn't recognize. The room was orderly—aged but well kept. In the corner, a pile of silk velvets and brocades covered in heavy, gaudy embroidery stood waist-high. She pushed herself upright, eyes darting to every corner.

An old woman with white hair pulled into pinned pleats sat before a fire, focused on a large boiling pot that emitted the most perfect smell Estella could remember. The bard's stomach grumbled, crying out for food beyond the moldy bread and stale water she had subsisted off of in the prison.

The old woman chuckled, though her focus did not leave the flames. "Welcome back."

Estella rubbed her eyes, struggling to remember how she came to the cottage. "Who are you? Where am I?"

"You may call me Lyra." The woman rose, picking up a ladle and bowl. Stew splashed over the edges of the bowl as she scooped it. Humming to herself, she crossed the small room and offered the steaming meal to Estella. "You were brought here once they pulled you off the chopping block. I'm sorry you suffered a bit more for it than any of us intended. Our alchemist miscalculated the blast. You must be starving."

As if on cue, Estella's stomach roared with a gurgle, begging for the meal before her. She stared at it, unsure her body remembered how to consume unspoiled food that had not been nibbled by rats.

"We didn't save you to poison you." Lyra placed the bowl on a small table beside the bed and resumed her chores.

Estella took the bowl, blowing on it. The swirls of the steam altered their dance from her breath. She ate with careful purpose, feeling each bite of meat, each piece of potato replenish her. After a while, she spoke. "While I mean no offense, I find it hard to believe that you saved me."

Lyra laughed and crossed the room to sit beside her. "Well, I certainly could not have carried you here alone."

"How?"

The old woman motioned to the enormous pile of fabric. "The duke threw a fit and sent me home immediately to tend to his ruined clothing. The fool touched everything he owned before he washed the dye from himself. Gave us plenty of items to cover you with in the wagon."

"You work for the duke?"

"I was employed by the duchess. Once designed every kirtle she wore." Lyra gazed into the fire; her eyes narrowed with hate. The light flickered across her features, softening them as if she were twenty years younger again. "The duchess never wanted much, always preferred her wealth to be spread to her people. But I could at least give her my time. The duke on the other hand…"

Estella rubbed her neck, thankful it still held her head to her body in one piece. "… can't get enough of flaunting his power and wealth."

Lyra went silent, picking up a pair of hosen from the foot of the bed along with a small knife. She stretched the biased fabric until the seam was where she needed it and plucked at the thread with the knife. "Took me a full day to get all of the orange out of these fabrics. My own doing at that."

Estella nodded at the garment. "What *are* you doing?"

"My part." With a sly grin, Lyra released the hosen, admiring her handiwork.

"Well, thanks, I guess." Estella stood up out of the bed. "I'll be going now."

Lyra set the knife in her lap and placed her hands over it. "Just where do you think you're going?"

"Home."

"You realize you cannot do that. Your home was burned to the ground the day after they took you. The duke is still expecting your corpse."

Estella froze, her legs losing their purchase as her entire world crumbled down around her. "So, I'm as good as dead, then. You saved me… for what?"

Much to Estella's surprise, Lyra hummed again. Her voice was small but firm even as she opened her mouth to sing.

> There once was a man who was blue.
> He found out his wife wasn't true.
> He couldn't get hard,
> So she went for the bard
> And they sang "fuck the duke" 'neath the yew.

Any other day before she faced her own mortality, Estella would have been more than honored to hear a polite old lady singing her raunchy tavern tunes. But today, all she felt was rage. "I would just like to go back to my life as a humble performer, thank you very much."

Lyra turned to her with wrinkled lips pulled into a thin frown. "Maybe you could do that in another country, 'cross the mountains, or down the river's end. But if the duke finds you alive, you won't even have the chance to be a martyr. Your head will be rolling in some back alley for maids to find as they take out the trash."

Estella's legs gave out. Tears streamed down her face. "Why…"

"Help us remove Iren. You've already written our most

powerful anthems. Help us spread them to those that need to hear them."

Estella shook. She struggled to reason with the words that were just said. She'd never composed any song any rational individual would ever consider an anthem. They were humorous songs with the sole goal of getting laughs, and thereby coin, from men too drunk to return home.

Lyra placed her hand on Estella's shoulder. "If you would prefer, we can smuggle you out. Give you some money so you can start anew. We've done it before."

Estella threw her hands in the air, knocking away Lyra's sympathy. "You want me to write things to incite the populace to riot? That's not what I do. Want me to write a song encouraging the duke to try necromancy since he can't keep a mistress? Now that I can do. But this? This I can't."

Lyra looked away, a tear running down her cheek. She took a deep breath and gripped the small knife in her hands. "The true heir is alive. I want your help to set the stage, as you might say, for his return. You can't go back into the taverns here, and I wouldn't dare risk your life. But we can spread your songs."

The heir, the duchess's child from her first marriage, had been murdered the day the duchess died. Everyone saw the body paraded through the streets as it was brought to the tombs. Estella remembered the day, twelve years ago, clearer than she wished. "In one breath, you tell me I can't show my face and then ask me to perform a job I won't even get paid for? Let me guess, *we paid you with your life.*"

"What you were writing already fueled a revolution. Why do you think he sought your head? So what if your criticism was based on humor? It got our attention enough to save you. The words of a martyred ghost are bound to have power."

Estella's jaw dropped. "What?"

"I've spent many nights in The Sleeping Dragon and was there the night they hauled you off to the dungeon. He can't silence all of us."

Estella's world as she knew it was gone. What was a life lived from the shadows when all one knew was the light of the stage?

———

Lyra's heart shattered as the memories of sitting in The Sleeping Dragon Inn with Cyne flooded her every thought. A score ago, both of them worked side by side as lady's maids to Duchess Rose. Their last night together, they laughed and lived as if the future was theirs. Yet their world splintered apart as the dawn arrived and they found the duchess dead.

Her hands fidgeted, anxious to hold on to the intangible memory as they twisted the simple silver band wound round her index finger—the smallest of promises that she and Cyne would resume their lives together once the dark times had passed. Once it was safe for her to return with the child she smuggled out in the night to safety.

A dozen years later, they still hadn't.

The sound of the lively midday patrons singing poured from the open windows as she passed the tavern on her way to the castle.

> Bursting his knickers 'fore the king
> His surcoat did not hide a thing.
> The duke turned beet red
> For he's no good in bed.
> Just like the good bard used to sing.

As reluctant as Estella had been to assist, she had eventually come around. It only took her recognizing the chance to regain the life she yearned for once Iren was removed. The ample opportunities for revenge didn't hurt either.

The public clung to every word she wrote, not knowing who was behind the homage to the martyred performer. Rumors spread it was, in fact, Estella's spiteful spirit from beyond the grave.

Rumors so very close to the truth.

Lyra kept her head down as she worked every day for the following weeks, as she had for years since the duchess's death shook the land. Though the former noble's room held none of Rose's old belongings, it at least still held the one lady's maid left behind to lay the path for the others' return. In every corner, she found evidence of Cyne's presence. A glyph of peaceful sleep was etched on the ceiling above where the bed once stood. A rune of protection was carved next to the door, long scratched out by Iren's own magicians.

The door to the duchess's old chamber burst open. Duke Iren, his face as red as the setting sun, threw a pair of hosen at Lyra, knocking her to the ground. "This is the fourth pair to rip in the past week."

She pulled the putrid tights away from her, holding them out as she shifted to kneel. "My lord?"

"What nonexistent competence did my cursed wife see in you?"

Lyra kept her head down, bottling her longing and her pride back to where no one but she could reach it. "My lord, I am not your tailor. I simply wash your garments and embellish them. Perhaps…"

"As of today, you are. See that it doesn't happen again."

"My lord?"

He shrieked in fury. "Is there something in my words that you failed to understand?"

She shook her head. "No, my lord. I'll see to it."

The door slammed as the duke left, and her heart pounded against her ribs. The tailor was gone. Sweat beaded on her forehead as she tried to piece together just what that meant. He may have been murdered in his sleep or in the streets. The best case would be that he heard wind of the duke's displeasure and fled before he became the focus of the duke's histrionics.

At the end of the day, Lyra rushed home with sacks of damaged garments flung over both shoulders. After an hour of quiet mending, she broke the silence and told Estella about her unfortunate promotion. "We need another song. There isn't much time."

"What about?" Estella asked as she spun a quill through her fingers.

"The child is of age. One of the duchess's lady's maids, a capable witch in her own right, fled with him at her lady's command. She's kept watch with her sisters every day since. Waiting for the day Iren was ripe to be removed. Waiting for the day she could return to their home."

"And you've just been biding your time?"

"I do what I can. Not that anyone ever noticed." Lyra stopped herself from going further into the details. No one outside of the courts ever cared that a noble dared to wear richer garments than the king. Even mages never noticed the small witch-runes of misfortune she would weave with beads and gems, not that she could imbue them like Cyne. "The scene needs to be set for his return. Iren has no claim to the throne as long as there is an heir. But he claims to have killed the child."

Estella rubbed her temples. "No one's going to go against his claims."

Lyra laughed. "You cannot be serious."

"Of course I am!"

"My dear child, what matters is what the people believe. If his credibility is destroyed, if the people believe the prodigal child will return and then he does, the transition will already have happened. Iren will have no chance to keep a power we already stripped from him. The people already believe that you're still coming after the duke from the grave. The truth's tendrils run deep in our consciousness. We only need something to hint at it to see it."

"I cannot believe you've talked me into all of this. But even I can't deny how much more well-known I am in death." Estella snatched a sheet of paper as she laughed and began to work.

> Their marriage, of course, was a lie
> And time proved she couldn't get by.
> And as for her child,
> Stashed away in the wild,
> Know the rightful's return is now nigh.

———

Estella left the seamstress's house for the first time in months and wandered the crowded streets. Not a soul recognized her, for who knew to look for a dead woman among the living? She made her way through the commotion and found Lyra with another elderly woman beside her, their fingers woven together as if the world might suddenly tear them apart.

In the past two weeks, rumors had consumed the duchy that the true duke lived and was returning to rescue them from Iren's cruel reign. And when he did, he was welcomed with open arms.

A hushed awe fell across the courtyard. The duke, still

dressed in his opulent finery, was marched by his own guards to the dais. Now, Estella would recognize Lyra's work anywhere. Motifs of grapes and blue flowers, none of which were native to this soil, were strewn across the black velvet surcoat. The work glimmered a harrowing call. From a distance, the details were beautiful. Upon closer inspection, they were perfectly reflective of a man who knew nothing of the land on which he dwelled.

The subtle details that Lyra had woven through every piece Iren wore since Duchess Rose's death had put the entire populace on edge in his presence. No one could ever place why they mistrusted him.

But now Estella knew.

She stood beside Lyra, proud to have befriended her. The three women stood stoic, watching the man marched to his death. Iren's head was slammed down on the very stump where Estella's had been months ago.

The people cheered. The crowd broke into song, repeating the words they had said over drinks since the true ruler's return.

Swarmed by truths, the duke is now through
Unite the people, not the few.
Call for help if you will
Knights still think you're swill.
If only you'd seen this plain coup.
Today, Iren sees his last morn.
I'll answer the calls of the horn.
Revolution! We cry,
Even nobles can die.
Nobody will miss him or mourn.

# THE MAGIC OF COLOR

## J.L. MILLIGAN

**M**y world, dreary and gray, changed the day the traveler came.

She stepped into the market square, a glorious conflagration of color made all the brighter surrounded by soot-stained walls and rain-blackened paving stones. The grime covering the city refused to mark her oddly puffy pants, leather boots, or her richly colored skin.

I stared at her, astounded. I had no words for the colors she wore. Didn't know the name for the teal of her doublet, the yellow revealed by her slashed sleeves, or the shade of her pointed, floppy-brimmed hat that existed somewhere between pink and purple.

And the pouches! On her back, pouches covered a bulky traveler's pack. They hung from hooks and rings and tied to crisscrossed straps, each smudged with a different color.

The meager crowd in the marketplace parted wordlessly before her as she strode with brisk, bouncy steps toward the lifeless fountain at the center of the square. Hopping up on the fountain's rim as if her massive pack weighed nothing at all, she pushed her hat back and spun a slow circle. I knew what she saw. In the not-too-far distance, the looming Lord's Wall stretched across the width of the city, partially blocking the view of the mountains. Buildings once white now washed gray and grayer with streaks of black. Black stones. And people wearing gray clothes with gray faces.

She stood on the fountain rim and looked at us, the citizens too young, too old, too weak, or too crippled to work in the mines, the factories, or the mills. There weren't many of us, and quite the sorry lot we made.

I wondered if we looked as strange to her as she did to us.

For one brief moment, the traveler's eyes landed on me where I sat on a ratty blanket, a collection of repurposed trinkets scattered around me, and I thought she smiled. Then she hopped off the fountain, unshouldered her pack, and dropped to one knee beside it.

The traveler rummaged inside her pack and emerged with a large gourd. She gave it a shake, then worked the cork free with a loud *pop* that bounced between the buildings bracketing the marketplace. That was when I noticed the unusual hush. The traveler held everyone in the marketplace in her thrall, and I don't think she even realized it.

I hesitated, unwilling to leave my precious goods untended, where anyone with a quick set of fingers could make off with them. But I wanted to see.

"I'll watch your stuff," the woman manning the food stall next to me said. "Go on with you."

Offering her a quick, grateful grin, I scrambled to my feet and limped my way through the crowd, pushing to reach the front. I wanted to see everything.

Humming an unfamiliar tune, the traveler gave the gourd another quick swirl, then slung its contents across the ground. A chorus of gasps rang out from the watchers, followed by a refrain of startled exclamations. Where the milky white liquid touched, the grime and soot vanished, revealing the pale gray of the cobblestones.

The traveler bent to study the cleaned section with a critical eye. With a happy sound, she sloshed out more of the jar's contents, then straightened and glanced around.

"Does anyone have a broom I might borrow?"

Someone did.

The traveler worked, using the broom to push the white liquid across the stones. Word of her arrival spread, and by the time she'd finished cleaning a large swath of ground before the fountain, the crowd had swelled with the curious until the marketplace was packed to bursting.

She held a thumb up in front of one eye, the other squinched shut. She held her tongue caught between her pretty lips in concentration. She tipped her head one way and her thumb the other. Her narrow nose wrinkled, relaxed, and wrinkled again.

"She's measuring," one old miner muttered to his neighbor.

"But for what?"

No one had an answer to that. No one even hazarded a guess.

Satisfied at last, the traveler gave a firm nod, plucked a pouch smudged with color—"cobalt blue," the old miner whispered, awed—tugged the neck open, reached inside, and threw a handful of its contents into the air.

Cries of shock replaced the crowd's barely repressed whispers as a cloud of color burst into existence. The traveler motioned with her hand, and the cloud rippled and moved, flowing to follow the shape of her gesture. Then she dropped her hand, and the brilliant blue dust settled to the clean cobblestones, as vibrant and stunning against the ground as the stranger against our gray-clad dreariness.

"Magician," someone whispered, barely louder than a breath.

I swallowed hard, fear a twisting knot in my gut. Not because the traveler used magic—all the stories said magicians had little magics and never hurt anyone—but because of the color. The traveler must not know—how could she know? If she knew, she never would have set foot in our city.

No one living outside the boundaries of the Lord's Wall could use color, or wear color, or own items touched with color. It was the Lord's Law.

But no one stopped the traveler as she pulled more pouches from her giant pack, each one containing a different pigment, rich and unique, that she then threw into the air. And she danced. Oh, how she danced. She spun and jumped, leaping from one side of her canvas to the other, scattering a rainbow of hues in her wake. She encouraged the crowd to clap to the beat of the silent song she moved to and laughed at her mistakes.

I saw smiles on faces I had never seen smile before. Pain and despair faded in the face of the traveler's unfettered joy as she created something entirely new and unknown. From the once blackened stones emerged a couple, dark of skin and hair, clothed in vivid red, caught in a flurry of motion as they spun together.

The traveler stood back to survey her work. Satisfied, she dusted her hands, gathered up the scattered pouches, and returned them to their places on her pack. She shouldered the pack, then turned to face the crowd. Beaming, she removed her hat in a sweeping bow, and the crowd clapped and cheered and laughed—actually *laughed*—and then she strode away.

———

I stayed in the market square for a long time, staring at the painted couple from the relative comfort of my threadbare blanket. I picked up one of my creations, turned it over in my hands, and slid out a hidden panel to reveal my little defiance. My secret act of color. My art.

I'd pieced together shards of colored glass—dredged from the river near the base of the Lord's Wall—inside a wood frame. The colors didn't form a picture. I hadn't arranged them in any particular pattern. I'd simply chosen the pieces that fit together best.

Glancing at the vibrant display painted onto the paving stones in front of the fountain, I slid the secret panel back into place and returned the trinket to its place on the blanket.

I'd been so proud of my creations, but now I'd had my first taste of true art. It simultaneously made me drunk with joy and sick with longing.

———

The traveler gave us other gifts, both large and small. Drawings sprouted all over the lower city, tucked into the corners of alleys and hidden in the shadows of doorways. Most of the images were messy scrawls in a single color that lacked the traveler's intent and skill. Other paintings—large things, depicting lives and scenes no one in the city had ever hoped to dream about, let alone seen—appeared overnight.

Bit by bit, the traveler changed our world. Workers on their way to the mines smiled at the bright yellow sun that greeted them on the city's wall. Children laughed and giggled as they crawled on and around everything, hunting out secret surprises—or making their own.

Old grandmothers sat on the fountain rim, their feet kept carefully away from the dancing couple, and told stories about *before*. Before the Lord came and built his home high up on the hill. Before a wall divided the city into those deserving of color and those who worked. Before the mines opened, and the factories and mills filled the sky with soot to stain the whole city black.

Before color became a forbidden thing.

I listened, gobbling up the stories no one had previously dared utter. I made a point of visiting each and every one of the traveler's gifts while I did my scavenging. For the first time in my life, I saw rainbows. And flowers. And birds. And creatures so fantastical they had to be plucked straight from the traveler's imagination.

I wasn't the only one to relish the discovery of such vibrant color and life in the world. I wasn't the only one to ask: "Why can't we have these things?"

Why must our world be flat and gray and black and lifeless? Why couldn't we wear fabrics dyed blue, or brown, or green? Why had the Lord stolen all the color?

How could we get it back?

———

My clubfoot spared me from the mines. I should have ended up in the factories, but my father ensured I didn't. I never learned how. He never told me, and I was too young to understand the danger he'd saved me from, let alone how. By the time I was old enough to ask, Soot Lung had stolen him from me, taking his answers with him.

Instead of joining the able-bodied population in hard, grueling labor, I created a job for myself. I held a certain sympathy for lightly broken things left by the wayside. I found those things and took them home. I cleaned them up, patched them, or broke them apart and made them into something completely new. Then I sold them at the market.

Eventually, I discovered a good place to find colorful secrets and started adding secrets of my own to my creations.

Now, I waded up to my thighs, my hands red with cold as I dredged the river where it passed beneath the Lord's Wall. The nobles tended to toss anything that wasn't perfect, and a lot of that dross ended up in the river. Shards of porcelain with painted flowers. Colored glass. Lengths of ribbon with frayed edges that hadn't lost any of their luster despite their dunk in the murky water.

I finished working free a box from the sludge at the river's bottom and gave it a quick shake to knock the muck loose. Lifting it out of the water, I turned it over, delighted with the find. Silver hinges. A small hasp, but no lock. Dark red wood that didn't look too damaged, beyond being slightly swollen with water. But the lid held the real treasure.

Colorful stones set into the wood created a simple, stylized insect—one with large eyes, a long body, and four wings—perched on a flower. The flower had lost one of its stone leaves, and several small crystals creating the faceted eyes were missing—likely the reason it'd been thrown away.

"That's pretty."

Alarmed by the unexpected voice, I shoved the box behind my back and jerked my head up to find the traveler crouched on the retaining wall of the opposite bank, watching me.

I hesitated but slowly brought the box back around. I ran my fingers over the stones and nearly knocked a petal off the flower. It *was* pretty.

"What will you do with it?" the traveler asked.

I ducked my head. Shyness had me stumbling over words until I gave up and lifted one shoulder in a shrug. Normally, I'd take it home, pry the stones and smaller crystals off the lid, then use them to decorate other things, but it'd be a shame to damage something so whole.

She gave me an odd look. "I didn't mean to startle you."

Blushing, I bent my head so the limp strands of my hair slid forward in a ragged veil. "It's okay," I mumbled.

"Dragonfly."

Curious, and a little confused, I peeked up at her. She gestured toward the box in my hands.

"The design. It's a dragonfly."

I resisted the urge to brush my fingers over the insect again, afraid of further damaging it. I mouthed the unfamiliar name, memorizing it.

After a long moment of silence, I risked another sneaking glance and braced myself.

"What you're doing, it's dangerous," I said.

She went very still for one breath. Two. Three. Then she pushed her hat back and scratched the top of her head, face twisted in bafflement.

"You mean my paintings?" she asked.

I jerked my chin in a barely-there nod.

"Why?"

"It's against the Lord's Law. You should leave before they punish you."

She snorted. "For what? Defacing public property?"

"No," I whispered. "For the color."

The Lord might have forgiven her for wearing color—she was, after all, a traveler and unfamiliar with the Laws and customs of the city—but he couldn't forgive the art. Not when it'd already roused questions and feelings in the whole city.

Dangerous things, feelings.

"What about you?"

Startled by the question—and the unhidden concern—I lifted my head, accidentally meeting her eyes. The intensity of her gaze caught me up like a bit of flotsam in a net, ensnaring me.

She tipped her head toward the box I held.

"That's against this Lord's Law, isn't it?"

I hugged the box tighter, hiding the dragonfly and flower—as if that'd keep them safe—and swallowed hard. I tried three times to speak but couldn't force my lips to shape any words, so I nodded again.

She studied me, eyes lingering on the box in my hands, and fiddled absently with the pouches tied to her broad leather belt.

"If a bird grows up in a cave, it will never learn to fly. It won't even know what it's missing because it's never known anything different. Don't you think that's sad?"

I frowned. "I don't understand."

Smiling a sad smile, she tugged a pouch free from its place at her belt. Opening the pouch, she shook some of its contents out over the water. I watched, breath lodged in my throat, as the blue powder hit the murky water and made it come alive.

"I think you're more like a dragonfly. Cave or not, you've taught yourself to fly. You just haven't experienced the freedom of open sky yet."

With that, the traveler cinched the pouch shut and rose. Before I could find the words that might keep her there just a bit longer, she tossed the pouch to me. It arced across the water, and I nearly dropped the box in my attempt to catch it. Juggling box and pouch, I managed to clutch both without dropping either or falling beneath the murky surface of the water myself.

"Nice catch," the traveler said.

She tipped her hat at me and started to leave. I took one hurried, sloshing step after her, nearly losing my footing on the slimy rocks.

"Is magic how you keep your clothes so clean?" I asked.

That wasn't what I meant to ask. I wanted to ask if magic was the reason the guards sent from beyond the Wall hadn't been able to wash away the painting in the market square.

Looking back at me over her shoulder, the traveler grinned —a thing full of mischief, secrets, and glee—and winked.

———

I carried the box tucked under one arm, the lid pressed hard against my side so no glint of color showed. My other hand I kept pressed over the pocket of my skirts where I'd stuffed the small pouch of pigment. Once home, I hid the box in the cache where I hid all the forbidden bits of color I found. That left the pouch.

Stepping into the small courtyard shared with six other buildings, I checked for watching neighbors before I withdrew my tiny treasure.

Blue. I had shards of blue glass, three blue ribbons, each one a different shade, and one unbroken porcelain dish painted with delicate blue flowers, but I had nothing like this. Pure pigment. A little leather pouch filled with infinite potential but a finite number of applications.

Despite knowing the name of the color, I didn't know the name of this particular shade. Didn't know if it should be used for water, or sky, or flowers, or something else entirely. I lacked a proper frame of reference.

In my world, the sky was black, gray, or darker gray. Sooty black painted buildings and stained the paving stones. I knew all the shades of flame and the red of blood from fresh to dry. But real color…

Carefully, I took a pinch of bright blue and rubbed it between my fingers. The smooth powder colored my skin.

Some crumbled into dust and sifted over my dirty apron. Lifting my eyes, I looked around the monochrome courtyard, searching. There, I decided. Up near the top of the wall, where the roof's narrow overhang offered some protection from the ink-black rain.

I grabbed the only chair I owned and shoved it against the wall. I tucked the pouch back into my pocket, leaving both hands free to clutch the chairback as I climbed onto it. My clubfoot throbbed, the chair wobbled, but I kept my balance as I slowly straightened.

I'd never seen a real flower, but I'd seen their depictions. On the dish tucked safely away in my hidden cache. On bits of embroidery from kerchiefs and ribbons lost to the river and found again. I'd seen the traveler's painted flowers scattered across the whole city.

I reached up and pressed my pigment-stained fingertip against the off-white of the wall. When I drew back, an imperfect blue oval remained.

A bubble of delighted laughter tickled the back of my throat. I bit my lip to hold it all inside as I brought out the pouch, touched my finger to the pigment inside, then smeared it on the wall, again and again. Five fingerprints clustered together in a lopsided circle. A flower.

Closing the pouch with trembling fingers, I tucked it back into my pocket and carefully climbed down from the chair. Only once I had both feet on solid ground—and after a quick check of the windows overlooking the courtyard to make sure I remained alone—did I throw my hands into the air and let loose a whoop of purest joy.

I looked to the crooked shanty that I called home, and my joy dimmed, but only a little. I imagined my father's laugh, his delight and pride at the little speck of beauty, and wished he were alive to see the magic I'd created with a bit of color.

———

I sat with my knees pressed against the wall, my clubfoot propped on the opposite leg to keep from accidentally crushing it into the rough cobblestone. Chewing on my lip, I leaned closer to the wall, so focused on trying to make a dragonfly with the last bits of blue pigment that at first I didn't hear the ruckus. Not until a crash sounded nearby, followed by a scream.

Startled, I jerked, nearly dropping the precious pouch. Guilt a heavy pulse in the back of my throat, I glanced at the mouth of the narrow alley. No guard stood there, come to arrest me for my illegal use of color. Yet the crashing sounds continued. So did the screams.

Heart sinking all the way to my toes, I quietly limped to the entrance of the alley and peeked out. Groups of men and women in shining metal armor layered over brightly colored tunics moved up and down the street. Pairs broke off to pound on doors, forcing their way inside whether the occupants let them in or not.

I shrank back as a pair broke off and started for me. No. Not me. The dilapidated apartment building I'd chosen to use as a canvas for my dragonfly. Moments later, I heard muffled pounding, the crack of breaking wood, then the distinct crash of crockery shattering on hard floors.

Realization struck me like an iron-tipped bolt to the heart. They were searching each and every house, every apartment, shanty, and tent. Looking for illicit pieces of color.

How many of my neighbors would suffer because they'd bought my repurposed trinkets, my pieces of secret defiance? What would happen to me if they found the cache buried beneath the loose floorboards of my hovel?

What would happen to the traveler if the guards caught her?

I hesitated. I should try to get to my shanty ahead of the guards. Gather my collection and dump it in the river to hide my crimes. Instead, I turned and hurried toward the market square. I would find the traveler and do whatever I could to keep her safe.

I wasn't the only one determined to help. I came out on a main thoroughfare and paused. A surprising number of people —workers and miners who shouldn't have been in the city at that time of day—crowded the streets, making a nuisance of themselves.

A laundress "tripped" and dumped an entire load of clean laundry at the feet of a guard. When he trod on a piece of clothing, she screeched and yanked it out from beneath him with enough force to make him stumble. Three broad-shouldered miners, pretending drunkenness, linked their arms together and staggered back and forth across the road, singing at the top of their lungs. Their dance did a remarkable job of blocking a group of frustrated guards.

Stifling a grin at the not-so-subtle signs of rebellion, I ducked down another alley and hurried on my way.

It seemed the entire city stood crammed into the market square. A stack of crates mostly blocked the entrance to my little alley, and I scrambled on top of them to get a better look. People stood cheek-to-jowl, their voices a low rumble of discontent. In the center of the square, balanced on the rim of the fountain, hands on hips, stood the traveler. A contingent of guards circled her, weapons drawn and readied.

"What your lord is doing is wrong," the traveler said hotly. She threw out a hand to indicate the assembled onlookers. "They are the beating heart of this city. Without them, the nobles stuck up on their hill would have *nothing!* How can you support a man who refuses them the simple joy and comfort of having color in their lives?"

The captain of the guards—marked by the bright-green plume of feathers sticking up from his helm—looked uncomfortable.

"The Lord makes the rules, not me," he said.

The traveler folded her arms over her chest. "And yet you're the one enforcing those rules."

He couldn't argue with her about that, and he didn't try. He gritted his teeth together and lifted one gauntleted hand to signal those under his command to take her.

That hand started to descend but stuttered to a surprised halt when a gooey, slimy mess hit his helm with a squelch. Dark-brown mud smeared the shiny metal, then dropped onto his pauldron with a plop. Vibrating with shock—and maybe fury—he turned to face the crowd.

"Who threw that?" he demanded.

A glob of something slapped the center of his back in answer. He didn't have a chance to turn, to search for the guilty party before another large mud patty hit him in the face. *Splat!*

Laughter replaced the low, angry rumbling of the crowd, followed by cheers as handfuls of muck—and other, less savory things—flew from every direction, pelting the guards. The traveler, up on the rim of the fountain for all to see, chortled with obvious glee.

With the guards so tidily distracted, she hopped off the fountain and into the crowd, which parted for her like water around a boulder, before closing in behind her, blocking the guards when they attempted to follow.

Abandoning my spot on top of the crates, I threw myself into the crowd and fought to reach the traveler before she broke free of the market square. I spotted her gloriously colorful garb amidst the drabness of the crowd and reached out, catching her by the hand. She whipped her head around, teeth bared in a fierce warning. Then she saw me and blinked in surprise.

"Dragonfly, what—"

"This way," I said, and tugged.

She didn't hesitate but changed trajectory to follow me.

"Where are we going?" she asked, a bit breathless.

"I'm getting you out of the city."

I didn't ask what had happened to her giant pack. I could only be grateful it currently wasn't on her back as we squeezed between the crates into the narrow alley and made our escape.

———

The riot in the marketplace spread throughout the city like floodwaters. The need to reclaim everything that'd been taken from them carried the people to the gates in the Lord's Wall and then beyond. Rage against the nobles—who had for years hoarded the finest foods and fabrics and goods, along with all the color—ignited the floodwaters into an inferno.

And everything within the Lord's Wall burned.

———

By the time we squeezed between the bars of the sewer grate and stepped beyond the city wall, my clubfoot burned like a coal in the fires of a smithy. The traveler looked bedraggled, her formerly pristine clothes marred with dirt and grime.

Still holding her hand—very aware of my sweaty palms and the chill of my fingers—we put our backs to the only home I'd ever known and started walking.

The traveler broke the strained silence first.

"Your limp. I noticed it back in the city, but..." But there hadn't been time to spare for things like worry. Not when escape had taken all our focus. "It's getting worse. Are you hurt?"

"I'm fine." Her blatantly disbelieving look made me smile, despite the pain. "I'm a cripple. I'm used to it."

She didn't look convinced, but she didn't push.

We passed the crooked dirt trail that went to the mines, and further still. Further than I'd ever gone before. She finally stopped, her hand slipping from mine to leave me feeling very alone.

"I'm sorry about your pack," I blurted.

She frowned, confused, then blinked and—to my surprise —laughed. It was a thin, tired sound, but it contained real mirth.

"Oh, don't worry about that. It's not the first pack I've lost. There's nothing in it that can't be readily replaced in other cities."

Other cities. My breath caught as yearning hit me like a punch to the gut.

"Thank you," she said. "For getting me out. Dungeons are no fun." She hesitated a moment. It looked as if she might say something else before she shook her head and changed her mind. "Guess I'll be going. I wish you happiness, little dragonfly."

"Criselda. My name's Criselda."

The tension carving grooves into the corners of her eyes eased, and she smiled, a thing brighter than the sun.

"I'm Amrin."

She dawdled, adjusting her hat, running her fingers along the straps of leather belted around her waist. When I remained silent, uncertainty and fear freezing my tongue, she sighed, offered me a fleeting grin, and took the first step on the road that would carry her far away from the city. Away from me.

"Wait! Take me with you!"

She reclaimed the step and turned to study me, expression solemn.

"What about your family?" she asked.

"Gone." I swallowed, grief a hard knot that never really went away. "My father died a month ago. I don't... without him, I'm alone. There's nothing here for me."

Amrin tilted her head. "You want me to take you to a new city? It'll be quite the journey."

"No." Frustrated, I wiped my hands down the front of my skirts, heedless of the mess I smeared across the already ruined fabric. "I want you to teach me how to do what you do."

A tiny frown puckered Amrin's brow, and my heart sank when she shook her head.

"That could take a long time. It takes practice and dedication, and that's assuming you have an aptitude for the magic."

"No," I whispered. "I don't care about the magic. I want to make art."

Her gaze raked over me again as if she'd never really seen me before. When she didn't immediately refuse, hope bloomed in my chest, a small bud, tightly furled and easily damaged.

"I travel constantly," she warned. "You might never have a real place to call home again."

"I don't care." The truth of it surprised us both. "I want to experience all the colors in your pictures. I want to make pictures of my own. I want to share those pictures with others."

I wanted to share a bit of ordinary magic with those whose lives lacked any.

After a long, long time, Amrin's lips twisted up into a beaming, delighted smile.

"All right, then. Let's go."

She held out her hand. Fingers trembling, barely daring to breathe, I clasped my hand to hers. Amrin pulled me forward, onto a new path, leading to an unknown future.

I laced our fingers together and squeezed cautiously. She squeezed back. I might not know what the future held, but one thing I did know. Wherever I went, my world would be full of color.

# BLEEDING HEART

## ALEXIS HANSEN

Paint splattered Fal's fingers in a spray of red and decorated the metal skin of the beast in front of her. She paid no heed to the mess, brushing her bangs aside and unintentionally coloring her braided auburn hair in the process.

There wasn't enough red.

Loath to leave her project, she pushed the rolling table of assorted colors away and searched the cluttered workspace, cursing herself for her lack of organization. Tinkering tools lay scattered everywhere, having been placed on whatever surface was closest once she was done with them. Useless enchanted wands and discarded potion samples were stuffed in every nook and cranny where they wouldn't be in the way. Parchment letters she hadn't thrown out yet filled a table and spilled onto the floor, each wax seal still unbroken.

Finally, she found what she was looking for. Picking up the jar of carmine powder and a bottle of flax oil, she brought both items to a granite slab and set to grinding the two together, relishing the strain of her muscles as an outlet for the rage simmering beneath her skin.

Creating things used to be a calming endeavor, when she'd done it for no reason other than she'd merely wanted to. When she could entertain hobbies and passions, she would get lost for hours or even days in the motions of her craft, fixated on getting the details just right. Time became but a wisp of air, imperceptible in its passing.

And Niss was always there to pull her out of it, gentle words reminding her to eat, gentle hands leading her to sleep.

With a shout of rage, Fal slammed the paint muller onto the slab. Then she sagged against it, drained, smearing more red pigment onto her elbows.

Now, there were no hobbies or passions. Just retribution.

Golden light permeated the workshop, lines of shadow twisting together on the stone floor from the window's tracery. Dust danced in the air in front of her face, and the silence bore down on her. After a moment, Fal pushed herself back up and shuffled to the arching window.

Her tower offered a stunning view of the verdigris forests and rolling foothills. A brook cut a path through the garden below and weaved beside a lone dirt road that stretched from her door to the distant snow-capped mountains that separated her from the rest of the kingdom. Her own perfect little world. Quiet, peaceful, and far away from everything else.

The letters lay on the table, their presence burning away at her awareness, trying to drag her back. Apparently, she hadn't gone far enough.

Yanking the heavy velvet curtains shut, she waved a hand, sparks of magic flying from her fingertips. The mounted oil lamps burst into flame, as did the chandelier of glass and tin, casting a hot glow across the room. Another handwave, and the muller sprang to life, continuing to grind the batch of unfinished paint on its own.

She pressed the button on a fist-sized device as she passed

its shelf, listening to the static that filled the room as she returned to her latest project.

The beast's girth took up at least a quarter of the room, towering over her, welded fangs glinting in the firelight. There was more work to be done, so she picked up a fresh brush and dipped it into a container of blue. Looping swirls spread across the metallic canvas under her touch.

Footsteps rang out behind her—ten steps, then a pause. A woman cleared her throat.

"It never ceases to amaze me, being in here," Niss said, as soft-spoken as always. "I love seeing what you create. Your art is beautiful."

Fal struggled to see what she did as art. It was a craft, a skill, one that could be developed and explained. Craft could be studied, broken down into techniques and calculations. If something went wrong, she could fix it.

Art was alive. It had a soul. People could spend centuries speculating on the meaning behind it, but no one could ever say for sure. Did it matter what was said by the artist? Or was the importance in how it was interpreted by the viewer? Did art require meaning? Couldn't it just exist?

Either way, art couldn't be wrong because wrong didn't exist in art. Fal couldn't understand it.

"I know you don't wish to talk to me right now, but I needed to say something. This time, I need to speak as a politician—no, a *citizen*—not your friend. Firstly, I must thank you, Amity Magus. Sorcerer of Peace. Iron Tigress."

Fal's grip tightened on the brush as Niss listed her many titles. She hated all of them. She hated that tone of voice most of all. Niss had never been so formal with her before, not since the day they'd met in her parents' gardens. One girl hiding away from a new and terrifying responsibility to the world, the other from a responsibility to the family name she'd borne her whole life.

"You have served the kingdom for decades, restoring peace to the lands time and time again. You alone hold the power of the cosmos, and never have you used it for ill will. You are, at the very core of your being, good."

Blue slashed across black metal, the brush skittering across the floor. Fal's jaw clenched, but she knew it was pointless to speak.

She wasn't *good*. She hadn't meant to do any of those things, never intended to become some powerful wizard. She certainly wasn't a hero. She'd just been in the wrong place at the wrong time. Everything that came after was only a result of people piling their grievances onto her.

She was weary of fixing everybody else's problems.

But now, she was angry.

The red was still gone. Orange was close enough, so she dipped her fingers in, forgoing a brush. The new color joined the dance of reds and blues around harsh angles and geometric edges, covering the chalk outline of her sketch.

"Secondly, I respect your position as a neutral party. You have solved so many disputes by looking at both sides and bringing them to a compromise. I believe you can do it once again. Thirdly, I sympathize with your desire to remain isolated from this conflict, to let the people learn how to sort this out on their own." Niss's words remained steady. "But I disagree with your decision to do nothing."

Easy for her to say. Lady Niss of the Dahlia had grown up around politics, watching her family make the decisions from the safety of their white halls. None of them had to experience the grime-covered streets, living with those decisions. They didn't have to see the street rats suffering the injustices those decisions inevitably brought.

Fal couldn't do it anymore. For decades, she'd done something, and yet nothing had changed. There was always more to fight about. Someone wanted to pursue progress, someone else wanted preservation. Someone wanted control, someone else wanted freedom.

War after war. Screaming voices in a sea of screaming voices. It never ended.

"We are on the brink of a civil war. This rivalry between Regina and Brackwater is growing hostile. If it isn't resolved soon, it will lead to bloodshed. There will be nothing but pain and suffering, and if you have the power to prevent that, shouldn't you?"

Fal's throat tightened. One of the swirls dripped where the paint had been piled on too thick, a blue tear staining the wrought iron.

The thing about art was that it was easy to get attached. It made you want to clutch it tight to your chest because it was an expression of you, something that contained your heart. If you left it exposed to the world, threw it to the wolves, they would tear it apart and leave nothing but an all-consuming abyss behind.

Craft was different. You could create a hundred prototypes and toss each one aside like it meant nothing, because the purpose was to build and to learn, to improve upon the next one.

So which was better?

A sigh escaped Niss's lips, a breath that was there one moment, gone the next. "I won't push you to go, but I intend to lend my services. Like you, I will remain neutral and assist in repairing what has broken. Maybe, even without you, we can prevent this war."

Did one have to be better? Could one exist without the other?

"I leave tomorrow with the merchants. You won't see me before I go. That's why I wanted to record this. Though we may not agree on this matter, I don't wish to leave on bad terms. Whatever happens, I look forward to the day I can see you again."

A click sounded, and the recording stopped, leaving Fal alone in the silence once again. Niss always did have a bleeding heart. Fal should have done whatever it took to convince her to stay. Should have gone with her.

She stared at her creation and the colors adorning it. The blue that drowned her grief, the red that brandished her pain. The orange that flared out like an explosion. Only one thing left to do now.

Before she could retrieve the new batch of red, the letters grasped her attention. She pinched one between her fingers, staring at it in contempt. Half of them were adorned with the Golden Stallion crest of the reigning faction, Regina. The rest bore the Wolverine of Brackwater, those intent on over-throwing the governing body. Both begged her to take their side, to end the opposition in one fell swoop.

The letter burned as she held it, flames curling the edges and turning them black. She dropped it onto the pile and watched as they all flared. Eventually, they died out, consumed by ash.

Gathering the red paint onto her palms, Fal imbued it with magic and approached the giant metal tiger, standing between razor sharp claws held on by nuts and bolts. The mechanisms within were crafted to perfection, pistons woven together with gears and covered by heavy metal plates. All protecting the keg of gunpowder contained within.

A message. One that couldn't be misunderstood.

She spread the red paint over the tiger's chest, forming a

bleeding heart that mirrored her own. Every ounce of magic she held poured into the beast.

Art was made better by craft, but it could exist on its own. The reverse was not true. Art permeated everything, brought life and joy. Without it, craft became soulless.

Niss was dead. She'd gone to help and instead got caught in the crossfire. If Fal was the craft, then Niss was the art.

The tiger came alive, stepping toward her and shaking off excess paint, stretching metal limbs and iron jowls. Fal hadn't prevented this war, and now it was too late to avoid the loss that sank its barbs into her flesh like a diseased flower that couldn't be uprooted. But she would end it.

Regina and Brackwater had failed to convince her to choose a side, but they succeeded in forcing her into this fight. They would regret it. They would see this symbol of the Iron Tigress and know who sent it. They would see the dahlia painted across its flank and know why. Then, they would see nothing.

There wasn't enough red. Soon, she would paint the whole city with it.

# YOU SHOULD NOT BE

## C.R. LANGILLE

She had been someone once. Full of power. Full of focus. Many feared her wickedness and did their best to avoid her very presence. Then, there was darkness. A sinking darkness that consumed, only to regurgitate and consume again. She floated in that black, lightless sea for what felt like eons, until her thoughts and memory faded to nothing and she was nothing.

Then there was pain.

It started in her throat, as if she had swallowed a thousand nails. Each breath came ragged and forced. Yet underneath the pain was elation. For she was alive when she should not be.

She sat upright, clutching her chest and coughing. Night had fallen, and only the single pale streak of moonlight punched through a hole in the castle wall to light the gloomy room.

That made her narrow her eyes, even through the excruciating struggle for air. Why was there a hole in her castle? She knew this place was hers, even though she couldn't recall her name. Yet, that fact, and the fact that the land was hers, was crystal clear in her mind. That wasn't the only thing she could recount... no, she could remember one other fact that settled in her marrow. She was a witch.

Not some potion-brewing hedge-witch. No, she was a *Witch*. One of the four. One to be feared.

So why was it that the darkness filled her with dread?

The Witch tried to stand, but as she did, her joints popped and groaned. The very act of movement was agonizing. She finally made it to her feet, but the world spun in circles. She steadied herself by bracing against the wall, but as she did, the darkness closed in on her.

The Witch could no longer see to the corners of the room; however, there was something there. The hairs on the back of her neck tingled as she stared into the dark. Then, whatever it was moved. It scraped against the walls with a sickening slap of something wet against the stone.

Somehow or another, the Witch had escaped the darkness, and deep down on some basic level, she knew that wasn't allowed. She should not be.

The darkness had come to reclaim her.

She shuffled toward the beam of moonlight, fully aware that it was the only thing now that could offer any mote of protection. The shadows slithered and wriggled, closing in on her, and she couldn't help but wonder why she had awoken like this, ripped from the darkness only to end up in a place ruled by the same.

As the wet thing slapped against the floor, only feet away now, the Witch took a step back and nearly tripped over a bucket that had been haphazardly dropped upon the ground. Upon seeing it, memories flooded the Witch's mind. She had tried to steal some stupid little girl's shoes... No, they weren't hers. Those silver shoes had belonged to another Witch. The Witch of the East. But in the Witch's attempt to get the shoes, that brat had doused her with water from that bucket.

Instead of claiming her prize, she had melted alive and felt every excruciating moment of it until the merciful darkness had taken her.

Merciful darkness indeed. How naïve she had been.

The thing slapped closer, and for half a breath, the moonlight illuminated a slick tentacle that was the color of a swamp at midnight. When the tentacle graced the moonbeam, it bubbled and boiled and let out a squeal that made the Witch's ears ring.

She snatched up the bucket and focused her will upon the brittle edge. Trees had a long memory, and though this particular tree had never felt the embrace of a conflagration, all one had to do was to ignite the passion and kiss of heat. The Witch concentrated on the wood, remembering what it was like to hold a torch aloft with the flames dancing their waltz.

That was all it took.

The bucket blazed to life with blue fire, illuminating the room and casting the shadows into a chaotic frenzy. The tentacles, caught in the light, seized and shuddered upon the floor. Blisters broke out upon the creature's countless slimy appendages, and the room filled with a high-pitched mewl that drove the Witch to her knees.

The tentacles appeared to collapse in upon themselves, shrinking smaller and smaller. With a juicy pop, they exploded and covered the floor with a black ichor.

The Witch fell to the ground and scrambled until her back was against the wall. She was sure more of the things would come and kept the flame held out in front of her. Amazingly, the fire didn't eat the wood at all yet stayed ablaze, and so she sat until the sun rose and filled the room with natural light.

With the shadows banished to the darkest corners of the area, the Witch could relax. The room was familiar to her—it used to be the kitchen. It was here she experienced her final moments, brought low by a simple bucket of water.

She growled and kicked it against the wall. With the bucket out of the way, she noticed a pile of moth-eaten clothes and a pointy hat. Her hat. The Witch looked down and found nothing covering her pale skin. She was as naked as the day she wriggled forth from her mother's greedy little womb.

The Witch took the clothes from the ground and shook the dust from them, causing an old black eye patch to fall from the bundle onto the floor. She put the clothes and hat on. The hat still fit perfectly, not that she expected any different. Once on, the stink of mildew and dust crawled up her nose.

"This won't do at all."

The Witch focused a mote of her will and snapped her fingers. The robes fluffed themselves, shaking the dust from them like they were a dog shaking water from its fur. Then, the blackness of the fabric turned blacker. The holes and tatters mended, and the stink turned into a nicer smell, one that reminded her of the forest in twilight.

"Much better."

There was one final thing. She leaned down, grabbed the old eye patch from the ground, and placed it on her head. With it on, she was complete once again.

With that taken care of, the Witch strode out of the room where she had so unceremoniously melted and made her way to a very special chamber. She navigated the halls and corridors without fail and knew she could do so blindfolded in the dark with her hands tied behind her back. However, the very thought of walking these halls in the dark made her shiver.

The Witch took a deep breath and centered herself. She would not let fear so easily conquer her. No, she would find out why she had returned to the realm of the living and what had happened to her castle.

Mighty oaken doors stood before her, nothing but shattered and splintered remnants of what they once were. The very sight of it stopped her in her tracks. If the doors were broken, then the crystal…

The Witch rushed into the chamber and screamed.

Her crystal ball was nothing more than broken shards and slivers of obsidian glass that covered the floor. She ran towards the ornate stone pedestal upon which the ball had once sat. The splinters of glass cut the bottoms of her feet, but she didn't care. The pain gave her something to focus on. It fueled her rage.

Surrounding the pedestal were four desiccated corpses wearing frayed robes of pale yellow. Their bodies lay in spots around the crystal ball corresponding to the four cardinal directions.

Clearly, they had been practitioners of the craft; however, she didn't recognize the robes, nor the strange symbols written in blood that stained their chests. The longer she stared at the symbols, the harder it became to focus on any details, and the Witch swore they shifted into different patterns when she looked away, even for a moment.

"Who were you, and what were you doing playing around with my tools?"

She walked past the blasted heap of bodies to the nearby window and gazed out at the craggy peaks that surrounded her castle. The path stretched out, and she knew it would connect to the Yellow Brick Road, and the road would take her to the Emerald City. Perhaps there that buffoon, Oz, could answer her questions.

With her mind set, the Witch strode out of the room. Yet the pop and crack of bone and the shuffle of feet across glass caused her to pause and turn around.

The four bodies stood upright, surrounding the pedestal.

As one, their heads snapped towards her, and they all pointed out the window at the path. The Witch backpedaled out of the room, never taking her eye off the four robed figures. Something in her mind told her that to look away meant death.

Once they were out of sight, she exhaled. On her way out, she stopped at one of the supply closets. The Witch threw the bucket to the ground and retrieved a broom. It wasn't *her* trusted umbrella. No, that had been a focus for her power. The Witch knew she wouldn't be able to do as much with a broom, but hopefully, it would still serve her will in other ways. With her new weapon in hand, she hurried from the castle. It was no longer her home, and she was not welcome there.

After some time, the Witch came upon the Yellow Brick Road. However, the road wasn't as lustrous as before. Not that the Witch was complaining; she hated the dreadful yellow. The way it glistened in the sun and glittered. So brilliant and... happy. The road was different now.

It was repellant, almost revolting. The more the Witch thought about it, the more she decided it was unclean. That was the only word for it. As she stared at the road in front her, the color appeared to swirl in front of her eye. The movement made her head ache and made it difficult to breathe.

In the back of her mind, she saw twin suns setting on a lake of brackish water. A discordant melody burrowed into her ears, taking root before she could shake it off.

Then, as quick as it happened, it faded. The music echoed in the breeze until it was nothing more than a songbird's tune. The road stopped shifting and whispering until it was just a smoldering lane of blasted yellow. The Witch licked her lips and steeled her mind before setting foot on the damned road.

It wasn't long before the Witch found herself in the forest. While the land seemed different and out of place, there was a time, not too long ago (although she really didn't know how long she had been gone, so it may have been ages ago) that she found solace strolling through the trees. She had loved how they would watch her as she walked through them, muttering her machinations. However, now they didn't so much watch her as stare through her, as if she weren't even there to begin with. The trees themselves held blank expressions, lifeless. If it weren't for the yellow glow in their eyes, she would have sworn that the trees were dead.

With no other choice, the Witch continued. Soon, the sun began to set in the sky, but the way the last bit of its rays danced with the branches was odd. The shadows crawled at odd angles, angles that made her queasy. She glanced into the sky and gasped.

There wasn't just one sun.

There were two.

Twin suns blazed with a sickly yellow glow, painting the sky with a grotesque palette of reds and pinks that looked more like the viscera of a dead animal than anything else. The Witch took a few more steps, still staring at the horizon and the abysmal suns sinking low in the distance. She wasn't watching where she was going and ran into something cold, wet, and furry.

The Witch let out a scream and fell backward, landing hard in the dirt. In front her was a large creature, almost twice as tall as her. She scrambled away on all fours and snatched up her broom. With her wits about her once again, it only took a moment to ignite it and bathe the area in cool, blue firelight.

The creature in front her wasn't as tall as she had first thought. It was high in the air, but it was hanged from its neck. A length of hemp rope creaked and groaned as the body swayed from the Witch's impact.

The creature itself used to have golden-brown fur, but it was so covered with matted blood it was almost impossible to see. The Witch stood and brushed herself off. Then, with the non-burning end of the broom, she poked the creature to spin it around so she could get a good look at its face. Perhaps this was a bear, or a tiger, or... *oh my.*

The creature finally spun into view, and the Witch grimaced. It was Lion.

He was missing both eyes, leaving nothing more than bloody cavities. Someone (or something) had peeled Lion's lips away, leaving him forever snarling.

"Who did this to you?"

It was true that the Witch had once wanted to subjugate Lion and ride him. It would have amused her and added to her overall malice. She was wicked, but this was something else.

Pinpoints of milky gold glowed to life in Lion's eyes. He growled, a deep guttural growl that vibrated in the Witch's chest.

"*You...*" Lion said, although the word came out covered with writhing maggots.

The Witch took a step back and tried, unsuccessfully, to hide her trembling knees. She raised the broom as if it were one of the fearsome spears her Winkie Guards once carried.

Lion's eyes narrowed and he growled again. "*You should not be. You should not have come.*"

"Speak not in riddles, or I will burn you," the Witch said and brandished her broom.

Lion laughed, though it was more of a wet croak filled with things that burrowed and things that whispered. "*I would welcome such a release.*"

"Who did this to you? Speak now!"

Lion champed his teeth at the Witch. "*I did. The play did. The black stars did...*" Lion looked to the sky and his jaw went slack. His body sagged as gravity pulled him always towards the ground. *"You should not be, Witch. You should not have come. Once you see it and witness it in all its infernal glory, you'll understand. You should not be, and now his hour is at hand."*

"Who? Who is this mystery villain you speak of? No more nonsense!"

*"With both the East and West devoid of Witches, and when the Wizard departed Oz, it left a void. Something filled that void. Now, we are all servants of the King. Run while you can or you will find yourself in the folds of his tattered robes."*

The Witch narrowed her eyes and scowled at Lion. She waved him and his warning off. "Do not deem yourself worthy enough to cast orders at me. I go where I please, when I please, and I will meet this king you speak of, and he will pay for his transgressions."

With that, she walked past Lion and continued down the path. However, there came a snap and another growl. The Witch whipped around and found only a frayed length of rope swaying in the breeze where once the Lion hanged.

She took a moment to compose herself before moving on.

As the Witch walked along the Yellow Brick Road, the air grew heavy and thick. It was a strange sensation, one she was not used to, nor one she particularly cared for. For it covered her in despair, making every movement and even the act of breathing difficult to complete.

It was the middle of the night when she came upon a dilapidated, ramshackle structure of what once could have been a cabin in the woods.

The very forest itself had reclaimed the structure, as the roots of the trees burrowed through the windows like corpse-worms feasting on a bloated carcass. The Witch found a stump nearby and sat upon it for a moment of respite.

She peered into the sky, still amazed at the alien aspect of it all. These stars were not the same as she remembered. They were black things that burned with hatred and loathing as they crawled across the night's landscape. And the moons—the moons made her feel weak as they peered into her very wicked essence. The Witch shivered and pulled her robes tight about her chest.

The wind picked up and caused a paper to flutter, catching her attention. Nailed to the door, which had rotted away from one hinge and hung at a precarious angle, was a flier. Even from where she sat, the brilliant and decorative lettering scrawled across its length was visible.

She stood and ambled over to the house, now acutely aware of just how dark the interior of it was. As a precaution, she willed the flame to life on her broom once again, though it did little to fight the bleak gloom.

The flier continued to flutter, as if it were a trapped animal trying to get unstuck. The Witch used the broom's handle to pin it down so she could get a better look. It read:

Come and see
*The King in Yellow*
a play in two parts
one night only
The Royal Emerald Theater

The lettering was gilded in gold, printed on thick paper. There was more to the playbill; however, someone or something had ripped the bottom portion of the paper off.

"I saw it."

The Witch sucked in her breath and raised her broom defensively. The voice had come from inside the house. It was quiet and tinny.

"Reveal yourself!" the Witch demanded.

"I cannot."

More riddles. More games. The Witch had endured enough nonsense to last a lifetime. It was past time she made an example out of stubborn fools.

"If you cannot, then I shall. Behold, I am the Witch of the West!"

The Witch slammed the end of her broom onto the ground, and the earth shook beneath her. The battered door of the house blew to pieces as the blue flame flared brighter than the sun. Of course, it blinded her as well, but she hoped it made a statement.

Her eyesight returned quick enough, and the light from the flame pierced the shadows inside, revealing a wooden chair. Upon the chair appeared to be a metal barrel of some sort.

"Who is there?" she asked.

"You shouldn't be," the voice said. It came from behind the chair.

"So I've been told."

The Witch strode into the house. Dead leaves crunched underneath her, cracking like thousands of tiny bones as she picked her way closer to the chair. As she neared, the Witch circled around to the back side, ready to incinerate the unlucky fool who decided to test her. When she finally stepped around and saw who it was, she was at a loss for words.

The Tin Woodman's head dangled upside down, hanging onto his body in the chair by a thin shred of metal. His arms and legs were scattered to the four corners of the home. His eyes were gone, leaving empty holes in their place. Inside his chest were dozens of pieces of rotting meat. Upon further inspection, the Witch saw they were all human hearts.

"Tin Woodman..." the Witch said.

"I saw it," he said again. "I wish I never had. It was a terrible thing to undergo. The first act was nothing special, and I was going to leave. But as soon as the second act started, I could not. I saw it, and so will you. Though you should not be."

"The play?"

"I saw it. I saw it. I saw it. I saw it. I saw it. I saw it. I saw it. I saw it. I SAW IT I SAW IT I SAW IT ISAWITISAWITISAWIT…"

The walls appeared to close in on the Witch, and she couldn't breathe as the Tin Woodman continued to yell so loud and fast that she couldn't make out the words anymore. She ran from the house and tripped over a root in the doorway, falling to the ground. At the same moment, the Tin Woodman stopped speaking.

The Witch rolled to her side and peered back into the house. The Tin Woodman's body and head were gone, but the chair was still there. Draped across it was a robe made of tattered yellow cloth.

Something compelled her to stare at the cloth, and as she did, it moved ever so slightly. Whether it was the wind or something else that made that putrid cloth wriggle, she would never know, for she stepped out of the cabin and continued her journey down the Yellow Brick Road.

Her feet were covered in blisters, bleeding as she came to a great cornfield. Rows upon rows of dead, dried-out stalks yielding rotted husks of corn stretched on for longer than they should have. Crows and ravens circled above, and their caws filled the air with a chorus that was equal parts maddening and deafening.

She had no choice but to follow the road that cut through the field, and it wasn't long before she came across a scarecrow. After seeing what had happened to Lion and Tin Woodman, the Witch steeled herself, ready to confront whatever twisted monstrosity Scarecrow had become.

Yet, she wasn't ready for what came into view as she neared the figure.

It wasn't that idiot Scarecrow. It was a munchkin. Or rather, it had been a munchkin at one point. The Witch held no love for the munchkins, nor did they feel any love for her in return. However, she never would have wished this upon anyone.

The munchkin had once had curly blond hair; however, time and those creatures that prey upon carrion had taken their toll upon the munchkin's small form. Where rosy cheeks once had been was nothing more than sunblasted skin pulled tight across a skull. Stringy bits and strands of hair littered the munchkin's head, and its eyes had long ago become some bird's meal. Whoever did this had tied the munchkin up and secured his arms and legs with a length of hempen cord. The Witch walked past the poor thing and realized that whoever strung the munchkin up had also gutted him and replaced his insides with straw.

A piece of bloodstained paper was stapled to the munchkin's chest. It was another playbill for *The King in Yellow*. This one was intact and allowed the Witch to see what was on the bottom. It was a curious yellow symbol that resembled a three-sided question mark with three dots in the middle of it all. While she was familiar with sigils and glyphs, the Witch did not recognize this one, though it radiated with harrowing power.

The Witch balled her hand into a fist. Whoever did this would pay dearly, for Oz was her home. Wicked she may be, but nobody could destroy her realm and get away with it.

She turned to continue down the path and let out a gasp. Her gaze fell upon hundreds of munchkin scarecrows lining the Yellow Brick Road.

There was a faint pop from the munchkin next to her. The Witch turned and found the scarecrow was now pointing down the road towards Oz. A thunderous cracking noise boomed through the air as the rest of the munchkins followed suit, all pointing their lifeless fingers the same direction.

Towards answers.

The Witch set her chin and strode forward, hoping if anyone was watching, they wouldn't notice the tear on her cheek or the tremor in her steps.

The night dragged on longer than it should have. High above her, strange moons danced in the night sky with chaotic black stars that roiled with their own malevolent intent. They were like soulless eyes that gazed upon her with hunger.

Each step became harder than the next. By the time she crested the rise and the Emerald City appeared in the distance, the Witch could barely move. It was wrong. It was all wrong.

Before her wasn't the Emerald City at all. Some monstrous doppelganger had taken its place. Instead of the mighty towers (that only looked emerald if you wore those blasted green glasses that the buffoon, Oz, had created) that crested the horizon for all to see, twisted spires the color of tawny death replaced them. That city sat on the shore of a great lake that should not be...

*You should not be.*

... where only dry land once was. Yet, this city was not dead. Music played in the distance, a cacophonous, discordant noise, but still, it was music.

It pulled her closer. Begged her to come and listen. And she found herself wanting to listen. For there was something else in that music. Something she sought.

Answers.

The Witch stood upon bloodied feet, and putting one in front of the other, she made her way towards the dim city.

By the time she made it to the city gates, her feet were nothing more than bloodied meat. How she wished she had those silver slippers now. Yet, she persisted. She was the Witch of the West, was she not?

*You should not be.*

The gates were open and unguarded, but it would have mattered little, even if legions of soldiers guarded the walls. The Witch would not be stopped.

The streets were likewise empty of people; however, playbills for *The King in Yellow* littered the path and covered every square inch of wall. She followed the music until it became so loud it threatened to burst her eardrums.

When she finally came to her destination, the music stopped.

It led her to the Royal Emerald Theater, or rather, what used to be the Royal Emerald. The battered doors appeared broken from the inside as if a mob of patrons had busted free.

For a moment, the sounds of screams and growls flitted along the wind, but the noise disappeared as it had come.

The inside lobby looked like a great battle site. The furniture was in pieces, scattered across the room. The wallpaper was torn, and sections of the wall itself were missing, broken away, leaving behind jagged bits of splintered wood.

Standing at the threshold of the auditorium was Scarecrow. He had his back turned to the Witch, but she recognized his ratty clothing and ridiculous hat.

"You! Who did this?" she demanded.

Scarecrow stood silent but opened the door leading to the auditorium.

The Witch stood straight and walked towards Scarecrow. As she neared, he turned towards her.

He had no face.

In its place was a simple burlap bag. Blood stained the outside of the bag, and something pulsed on the inside.

"Who did this? Tell me!"

Scarecrow pointed to the auditorium. Inside, the seats were all empty except for three people sitting in the front row.

The Witch walked past Scarecrow towards the tiny audience. As she did, a spotlight turned on, illuminating the trio.

She knew them well, for they were her sisters. The Witch recognized Glinda's rich, red locks.

"Sisters! A sight for sore eyes. Tell me what is going on here!"

They did not answer. Scarecrow closed the door behind the Witch, and the auditorium was bathed in darkness apart from where her sisters sat.

The Witch's heart threatened to burst from her chest as the darkness embraced her. Just like before in her castle, there was something there with her. Something wet.

Something hungry.

The Witch willed her broom to light, and light it did, but its paltry blue flame did little to keep the shadows at bay. The pale glow flickered and shrank. The thing crashed into the seats behind her.

The Witch screamed and ran towards her sisters.

Whatever chased her was fast. The Witch channeled every bit of energy she had left into running. She was almost to the spotlight and her sisters when something cold and ropy wrapped around her waist. It tightened, blowing the air from her lungs and wrenching her into the dark.

———

When the Witch woke, she was in a chair. The first thing that came into view was Glinda's pink dress. She let out a sigh of relief and sat straight, turning towards her sister.

"Thank everything unnatural in this world, Glinda, what is—"

The Witch's words caught in her throat. She wanted to scream, but it wouldn't come.

Glinda was dead. No more than a dried husk, much like the corn in the cornfield—her face locked into an eternal scream of terror. What once was a beautiful, good Witch, was nothing more than a mummified shell, forever staring at the stage in terror.

The Witch leaned forward and found the other witches were the same.

Before she could rise and run for her life, the lights dimmed and the spotlight moved from the Witches to the stage.

A lone figure stepped onto the stage wearing a pallid yellow mask.

The orchestra struck an off-tune chord, chilling the Witch to the bone.

A presence loomed behind her. She dared not turn to look, but whatever it was, was ancient and powerful.

Tattered strips of yellow cloth fluttered in her periphery. She closed her eyes and looked away. Hands, as cold as the vast emptiness of space, gripped her cheeks and urged her to look on.

The play was about to start.

# ABSOLUTELY CHARMING

## MICHAEL A. STACKPOLE

I felt excited tremors of anticipation ripple through me as the postman took the folded slip of paper from my hand. The bored look of indifference in his flat eyes died beneath the wave of lustful hunger surging onto his face. His mouth hung open as his eyes devoured each word and his lips faithfully echoed them a second later. His eyes flicked from word to word, faster and faster as he neared the end of the paper, then he flipped it over, greedily looking for more.

When he saw he had read it all, he reread it quickly, and would have started on it a third time, but my hand closed on the paper. He tried to pull away, but I folded the sheet, hiding the writing from him, and he snapped out of it. Reluctantly he let me pluck the paper from his hand.

"My God, that's great!" He wiped his brow with a yellowed handkerchief. "Is there any more? There's got to be more. I mean, that's the best thing I've ever read. My God, you're a genius!"

I smiled in a kindly fashion. "Thank you, Carter. It's just a little thing I tossed off this morning."

The mailman gave me a low whistle. "Boy, I thought you

gave up writing five years ago, after that guy rejected your book. I mean, you know, I've not read your book, but if it's anything like this, that editor was a fool."

I forced my ire away at the mention of HIM and maintained the cordial facade on my face. "Yes, well, editors are known for momentary lapses in judgment. Perhaps he will see the error of his ways. Thank you, Carter, for your encouragement."

"Yessir, Mr. Daye." He pointed a trembling finger at the note in my hand. "When you get that published, let me know where. I'm gonna buy bunches of copies."

I contained my mirth until I'd shut the door and shot the bolts, then let it ring loudly within the confines of my dingy domicile. I crumpled the slip of paper in my left hand, then carelessly tossed it into the corner. I had succeeded! After five years of research, trial and testing, I had done it. I had discovered the secret, and now that I knew it, I would have my revenge.

I stooped and recovered the ball of paper, then smoothed it out against the cover of The Grand Albert. A simple, slender piece of ruled paper, it was unremarkable. It was actually less than that, this collection of words that imbecile Carter had seen as a great work of literature. Feeling the power surge through me, I started reading it aloud, "Clorox, assort. soup, rice - 1 lb, toilet paper," but my oration was subsumed by laughter.

The words meant nothing and would have been nothing if not for the device I had painstakingly inscribed at the head of the sheet and now hid beneath the ball of my thumb. This was what had taken five years of delving into arcane tomes. Elusive and deceptive, I tracked it through aged parchments that had not been touched in centuries. I waded through witchhunter diaries and forbidden books of lore in languages long thought dead but pulsing with power. A hint here, a clue there led me on my quest for a symbol of power, a symbol because of which men and women had perished in legions.

Ultimately, my quest was frustrated because all trace of the sigil I sought had been destroyed. Those who knew its power had learned to fear it, so they caused all representations of it to be destroyed. However, other sigils that had adopted bits and pieces of it to steal some of its power still remained. Like an archaeologist or a geneticist I tracked back to this Eve of arcane symbols. I stole a piece from the Key of Solomon here and the Enochian alphabet there. Little by slowly, methodically and scientifically, I synthesized the device I had so long hunted.

I brought it back from extinction.

I recreated the Siren Sigil, and I knew it was good.

Carter had proved it. Carter, my simpleton lab rat, had endured countless lists of nonsense as I tried out variations on him. Some provided curious and amusing reactions, but none, until this morning, had given me what I wanted. Carter, under the Siren Sigil's influence, gobbled up my grocery list like some tawdry thriller and could not put it down. He wanted more and, when there was none, read again what I had written. From that fragment he deduced I was a literary genius.

If it had worked on Carter, certainly it would work on HIM.

I crossed through the musty stacks of books piled like stalagmites on the floor of my front room and into the bedroom. Feeling invincible, I reached up and pulled the framed letter from its place above my bed. My spur, the thorn in my side, the driving force in my quest, this letter had haunted me since Carter had borne it to my door. Over the years, when despair had sapped me of strength and will, I'd reread it to fill me again with rage. Now, with victory in my grasp, I allowed myself the luxury of again reading of my humiliation.

"Dear Mr. Daye,

Under normal circumstances, as a common courtesy, I undertake to thank writers for sending their work here to Mountain Books. However, in your submission I find nothing that motivates me to do this. I do appreciate, in both your cover letter and Chapter 3, your expressing your opinion of the "substandard and puerile" work we have produced in our various lines. Repetition of that criticism in Chapters 7, 12 and 127 might be viewed as excessive, no doubt motivated by your belief that our "moronic editors" would be "incapable of recognizing subtlety if it jumped up and shot them with a nuclear particle accellerator [sic]."

I must agree with your assertion that your work is difficult to bracket, though not as you suggest "because literature, as a concept, is really too limited to encompass [your] work."

You are not Dostoevsky.

You are not Dickens.

You are not literate.

The novel you have submitted to us is useful only as a dictionary of mercilessly overworked clichés. I would call your characters cardboard, but I am not of a mind to insult cardboard. Elizabeth Taylor's entire wardrobe is less purple than your prose. The suspension of disbelief necessary to accept your tale is only exceeded by that which is required to believe we would actually consider publishing this work. If 50,000 chimps banging away on typewriters for years could produce Shakespeare, I would guess that 50,000 Hyram Dayes banging away on typewriters could produce an almost publishable CumQuik novel.

I truly hope this is the only novel you have attempted. If

not, I fear your home could be classed a toxic waste dump by the EPA. You should be reported to a Civil Rights Commission for sending this work out without a warning label and were the Nuremburg court still in session I would report you for human rights violations for producing this work.

If, by some twisted piece of logic (of which you are most assuredly capable), you do not understand that I suggest you cease and desist all writing, please do not consider Mountain Books a possible market for your work. The same goes for any and all relatives you have.

Wishing you were dead,

Gordon Cobb

Editor in Chief

I flung the frame from me and it smashed against the wall. Chuckling to myself, I reached up on my highest shelf and pulled down the box containing my manuscript. Lovingly I blew the half-decade's accumulation of dust from its lid. Setting the box down on the bed, I opened it and pulled the 600 page manuscript forth. Clutching it to my breast, I headed back out to my work table.

*Love's Chainsaw Caress* would finally see print!

I resisted the temptation to paint the Siren Sigil on the cover page. That page was superfluous and likely would not be copied were the manuscript duplicated within the printing company. Also, I assumed that were the sigil to exert its influence in the mail room, it would take forever for my manuscript to reach HIS hand. I turned to the first page and, in the wasted white space at the head of the Preface, I set to work.

Dipping my narrow brush in the bottle of black ink, I started to draw the Siren Sigil. With serpentine forms I created the lozenge device that encompassed the whole of the design and empowered it. Near the top I then added the triskell vortex that would draw the reader down into the work. Light shading and twists through the lines hinted at seductive feminine curves and the womb-warmth we all distantly remember and crave. This urged the reader on and reassured him that no matter what he read, nothing could be more right or perfect.

Strong, quick tentacles laced down from that and intertwined in a morass of Celtic knotwork. This firmly placed my work as part of reality and rewarded the reader with the knowledge that he was truly capable of adjudicating what was art and what was not. Clearly, in the reader's mind, my work deserved exaltation as the highest form of human endeavor in the world of literature and in all of art.

Finished, I resisted the trap of wanting to admire my own work. I had slipped an index card over the first half of the design as I worked on the second. I knew, had I allowed myself to succumb to temptation, I would have read through my book, and again and again until I fainted from starvation or someone physically tore me away from the manuscript. Three days of reading and rereading the TV Guide on which I'd idly doodled the sigil convinced me not to make that same mistake twice.

I returned the title page to its place, then put the cover letter I'd prepared earlier in the week on top of it. This time I refrained from giving HIM the benefit of my wisdom. In fact, other than a strongly worded suggestion to include the "design" on page one of the manuscript on the first page of the novel, my letter was perhaps the most banal thing I had ever written. I smiled because I knew there be time enough for other letters with yet other Sigils that would show HIM the error of his ways.

Carefully packaging up the manuscript, I hauled it down to the Post Office. I resisted the temptation to send it express, and relied on "Priority Mail" to get it to New York inside two days.

Revenge should be savored, I reminded myself, and an expressed manuscript would instantly send up a red flag. This would not do. I wanted HIM taken utterly unawares.

The next week was one of exquisite agony. I started and stopped a dozen different novels featuring Clint Kerage, the hero of *Love's Chainsaw Caress*. Countless were the times I'd picked up the phone to call Mountain Books, but I always hung up before HE could be put on the line. No. No! I would not tip my hand. The time to gloat would come later, when Caress had made me a fortune and I had HIM groveling at my feet at my hideaway on the Cote d'Azur. Begging for my next novel, HE would be and I'd tease him and lead him on, then deny him, lashing out with those words of his, the words I'd long since had burned into my brain.

Toward the end of the week I had resolved to buy, with the huge advance they would offer me, a video camera. I realized that the real money would be made with the movie version of Caress and I felt fairly certain the sigil would function, with some changes, in a film or video format. For a half-second I felt a chill as it occurred to me that some television executives might already know of my secret and have been using it for years. My sense of horror almost overwhelmed me, but I rose above it and vowed not to let others exploit my secret.

Then, on Saturday, Carter appeared at my door. I signed for the Express Mail package he had for me, then shut the door on his simpering whine for another look at what he had read before. When I told him I had destroyed it as unworthy, he wilted and began to moan. As I tore the package open the sound of his pitiful voice faded from my consciousness.

The letter was from HIM.

Obsequious is a delicious word that feels perfect in the mouth for spitting out with derision. To describe his letter with it, however, would be describing the sun as a photon or an ocean as a molecule. I read the letter as avidly as had Carter my grocery list. "Brilliant...unparalleled work of a scope and vision unimagined before...gritty and realistic, yet fantastic and allegorical...a genius for description, characterization and plotting...a masterwork from a Grandmaster of the English language."

Yes, yes, he said everything I expected and more. He had been shattered, broken on the anvil of his own ego. I'd sunk the hook in and gotten him. He said he was rushing the book into production and assumed I would find the enclosed contracts satisfactory. "Sign both, put them in the SASE, send them and we'll be in business."

He closed with, "Until I read your book, I had been an atheist. Reading your work has convinced me that God does exist and he has smiled upon you."

My own laughter ringing in my ears, I sat at my desk to look at the contracts. "the author warrants..." Yes, standard boilerplate. I hitched as I came to the clause in which Mountain Books retained all serial rights to the work, but I let that slide. I could not allow a magazine to use my sigil on a portion of the book lest millions of zombies be left rereading the excerpt without ever getting the full book. No, that would not do.

On, I read, faster and faster. The legalese flew past, seeking to entangle me in copious clauses, but I sorted them through. Then I hit another rough spot: no advance for the book! And another: royalties of .0001% of cover, due once a century, on the 29th of February! What was the meaning of this?

Further and further I raced through the contract. Outrage upon outrage was heaped upon me and my novel. Mountain Books retained all rights to foreign editions and book club editions, and had to pay me nothing! They demanded exclusivity from me, with a novel coming every 3 months, for as long as I lived. I would move to New York and live in their building and write for them, then whenever I perished, they wanted the right to farm my work out to any hack willing to work beneath my name!

My jaw dropped in utter disbelief. Here Gordon Cobb — HE — had proclaimed my work akin to that of something penned by God, yet some grasping flunkie in his legal department sought to deprive me of my due. Some little, empire-building munchkin with a sheepskin from South Bayou College of Law and Cosmetology, no doubt. Well, he would learn to rue the day he dared draft this mandate of involuntary servitude. When I got through with HIM, HE would be through with this moron!

In a fury I flipped to the last page of the contract and stopped cold. Gordon Cobb had already signed the contract. How could he have allowed this travesty to go out over his signature? Did he not know with whom he was dealing? Could he not see he was cutting off his nose to spite his face?

Then, down toward the bottom of the page, I saw it. I recognized the gentle shape of its triangular outline. The tendrils flaring off like black flames began to writhe as though fanned by an unfelt breeze. The uneven scales at its heart righted themselves as I tilted my head to study it. Its shape, its simplicity, its invitation to join the fold. It all made sense.

The Thrall's Sigil.

I picked up my pen.

Originally published in *Amazing Stories*, July 1991

# "TERRORISTS ARE THOSE PEOPLE WHO BUILD DEPORTATION PRISONS, NOT THOSE THAT BLOW THEM UP!"

## FROM THE BOSTON ANARCHIST BLACK CROSS

### WILLY PALOMO

It is said one ton of concrete can be ruined
      by pouring in five cups of sugar,
so for moments, I imagine the border wall
      defeated by Abuela's pan dulce.
I hurl conchas like grenades, keep a cuerno
      strapped to my waist, ready to fire
la caña mis primos carried off hilltops
      on bare shoulders. Picture borders
crumbling soft as De La Rosa's mazapan
      on mi lengua. I have always
had a sweet tooth. I have always hated
      the dentist & loved to poke holes
in the walls of a hater's imagination.
      Like you, I want to believe
the most bitter bigot can be crushed
      by a handful of mercy.
That one child's dream can bring
      a nightmare to its knees.
But so little sugar only slows the hardening
      of concrete. Before long,

even its sweet is petrified. The way
        a woman who has forgiven
a man too many times slowly turns
        to stone. I want to believe
there is enough dulce in my blood
        to stop the wall from setting.
That I won't have to slit your sweet
        throat for my cups of sugar.

# ABOUT THE AUTHORS

**C.W. Allen** is a Midwestern transplant to rural Utah, where she serves as the League of Utah Writers newsletter editor and the president of the West Desert Wordsmiths chapter. She writes fantasy novels for tweens, picture books for children, and short stories and poems for former children. Her middle grade novels *Relatively Normal Secrets* and *The Secret Benefits of Invisibility* are out now, with many more stories waiting in the wings. Follow her latest projects at cwallenbooks.com.

**Bradley S. Blanchard** has done several kinds of writing, both professionally and personally, across the years but always comes back to speculative fiction for both reading and writing, because he finds nothing more interesting than a good "What if" story. When he's not writing he's doing other stuff, because you can only stare at the wall for so long before the wall stares back at you.

**Abby Feenstra** is an author, long-distance runner, forever faithful 49ers fan, and dog/cat mom living in Salt Lake City,

Utah. She is originally from Reno, Nevada, where she graduated from the University of Nevada's English department. When she's not writing, you can find her in the mountains with either trail-running shoes or skis strapped to her feet.

**Alexis Hansen** grew up moving across the country before returning to her family's roots in Utah, where she's been raising goats ever since. She was homeschooled, spends way too much time lost in her own imagination, and can never decide whether to write or draw. She enjoys butting heads with her goats (not literally!), going on walks with her dogs, and fulfilling her honorable duty as a cat bed for her feline overlords. You can find her on Twitter @goatlextales

**C.R. Langille** spent many a Saturday afternoon watching monster movies with their mother. It wasn't long before they started crafting nightmares to share with their readers. They are a retired, disabled veteran with a deep love for weird and creepy tales. This prompted them to form Timber Ghost Press in January of 2021. They are an affiliate member of the Horror Writer's Association, a member of the League of Utah Writers, and they received their MFA: Writing Popular Fiction from Seton Hill University.

**Brooke Losee** lives in Utah with her husband and three children. She enjoys writing, gardening, rock hounding, and being a mom. Brooke appreciates the small town lifestyle and adventurous landscapes of where she lives, often using her background in Geology to aid in her writing. She has always had a passion for science, history, and of course, all things books.

**J.L. Milligan** is a hungering void for all things fantasy with a special love for the ridiculous, which at least partially explains her fondness for Japanese anime. She's a craft master and kitchen wizard, as well as a dabbler in various other art forms. Her current aspiration is to traditionally publish YA fantasy exploring love in all its forms.

**Margot Monroe** is a romance writer living in Salt Lake City with her husband, daughter, Italian Greyhound, and a flock of black-capped chickadees and lesser goldfinches in her backyard (along with a squirrel named Helen Squirrelly Brown). She's the Secretary for the Salt City Genre Writers chapter of the League of Utah Writers. You can find her at www.gowritemargot.com and @gowritemargot

**Willy Palomo** (he/they/she) is the son of two immigrants from El Salvador. In 2018, he graduated with an MA in Latin American and Caribbean Studies and an MFA in Poetry from Indiana University. In 2017, he received the City of Bloomington Latino Leadership Award and the MLK Building Bridges Graduate Student Award for his work serving undocumented communities in Indiana. He has taught literature, creative writing, and the Poetics of Rap in universities, juvenile detention centers, community centers, and high schools. He has performed his poetry nationally and internationally at the National Poetry Slam, CUPSI, and V Festival Internacional de Poesía Amada Libertad in El Salvador. His book reviews and creative writing have been featured in *Best New Poets 2018*, *Latino Rebels*, *Antologia de Posguerra*, *The Wandering Song: Central American Writing in the United States*, and more. He is a founding member of Plumas Colectiva, a literary and art collective of Latinx creators in the 801. He is the director of the Utah Humanities Book Festival.

**Talysa Sainz** is an author and freelance editor who believes life's deepest truths can be found in fiction. She runs her own editing business and spends her time at the library or volunteering with the League of Utah Writers. Always fascinated with the structure of words, she studied English Linguistics and Editing at BYU. She then went on to receive a Master of Science in Management and Leadership, focusing on nonprofit work, from WGU. Talysa is the President of the Utah Freelance Editors.

**Michael A. Stackpole** is the multiple New York Times bestselling author of over forty fantasy and science fiction novels, his best known books written in the Star Wars® universe, including I, JEDI and ROGUE SQUADRON, as well as the X-Wing graphic novel series. He has also written in the Conan, Pathfinder, BattleTech and World of Warcraft universes, among others. Currently the Virginia G. Piper Center for Creative Writing at Arizona State University Distinguished Writer-in-Residence, Stackpole's other honors include: Induction into the Academy Gaming Arts and Design Hall of Fame, a Parsec Award for "Best Podcast Short Story," and a Topps's selection as Best Star Wars® Comic Book Writer. Stackpole is the first author to sell work in Apple's App Store, and he's been an advocate for authors taking advantage of the digital revolution.

**Johnny Worthen** is an award-winning, multi-genre, hybrid, tie-dye-wearing author, voyager, and damn fine human being! Trained in literary criticism and cultural studies he earned his Bachelor's and Master's degrees from the University of Utah. Beyond English on a good day, he speaks Danish and reads Latin. He is a Utah Writer of the Year. An avowed

Deconstructionist, Johnny writes up-market stories from the inside out, beginning with theme and pursuing an idea through whatever genre will best serve it. So far he has published fiction novels as mystery, young adult, comedy, urban fantasy, horror and science fiction, both traditionally and independently. A frequent presenter and panelist at writing conferences and fan conventions, he is active in local communities of artists and writers. A long-time volunteer for the League of Utah Writers, the state's oldest and largest writing organization, he has served several high positions of leadership there, including President from 2018-2020. When not writing his own stuff, Johnny mentors, edits professionally, and teaches Creative Writing at the University of Utah as an Associate Instructor. He lives in Sandy, Utah with his wife, sons and cats. There's also a lawn.

**Bryan Young** (he/they) works across many different media. His work as a writer and producer has been called "filmmaking gold" by The New York Times. He's also published comic books with Slave Labor Graphics and Image Comics. He's been a regular contributor for the *Huffington Post, StarWars.com, Star Wars Insider* magazine, *SYFY, /Film*, and was the founder and editor in chief of the geek news and review site *Big Shiny Robot!* In 2014, he wrote the critically acclaimed history book, *A Children's Illustrated History of Presidential Assassination*. He co-authored *Robotech: The Macross Saga RPG* and has written two books in the BattleTech Universe: *Honor's Gauntlet* and *A Question of Survival*. He teaches writing for *Writer's Digest, Script Magazine*, and at the University of Utah. Follow him on Twitter @swankmotron.

**J.E. Zarnofsky** is a writer, larper, costumer, and all around fantasy enthusiast. She is always seeking new ways to tell heartfelt and collaborative stories. Apart from her day job in software, she can be observed in her natural habitats of coffee shops, ice rinks, or medieval(ish) battlefields—armored and ready with her sword or bow. Follow her online at jezarnofsky.com or on Twitter @jezarnofsky.

# MORE FROM THE LEAGUE OF UTAH WRITERS

## FIND ALL OUR ANTHOLOGIES AT LEAGUEOFUTAHWRITERS.COM

The League of Utah Writers    85th Anniversary Anthology

THE FUNCTION
OF FREEDOM

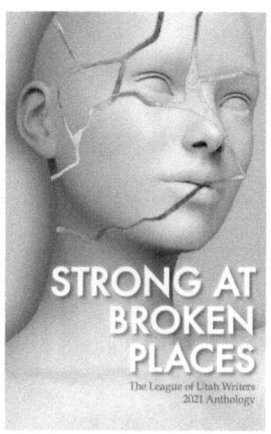

STRONG AT
BROKEN
PLACES

The League of Utah Writers
2021 Anthology

# WHAT CAN THE LEAGUE OF UTAH WRITERS DO FOR YOU?

*The League of Utah Writers is a non-profit organization dedicated to offering friendship, education, and encouragement to the writers and poets of Utah. Our organization aids our members in the improvement of their craft and support of their goals.*

The League of Utah Writers is a vibrant writing community with chapters throughout the state, as well as online with members across the country. Membership in the League of Utah Writers provides support and opportunities for writers and editors at all levels of their careers.

**Join us at www.leagueofutahwriters.com**

The
**Pre-Quill**
Conference

Pre-Quill is the League of Utah Writers' Spring writing conference - a day long event of classes, workshops, and networking with other wordsmiths.

This event showcases our local Utah writers in classes and courses geared to each unique voice and talent. It is also a great place to start working on stories, poetry, or any of the other categories listed in the Wooley awards - the League's prestigious contest awarded at the annual Quills conference each year.

Pre-Quill helps refresh your creative neurons with the pulse and energy only spring could bring.

Find more about The Pre-Quill Conference at
www.leagueofutahwriters.com

THE
QUILLS
CONFERENCE

The League of Utah Writers invites you to join us for the Quills Conference, hosted locally in Salt Lake City annually near the end of summer.

The Quills Conference is the League's premium event, bringing in special guest authors, agents, editors, and publishers from around the nation.

This four-day writing conference is for everyone from the fresh voices not yet published to the well-established writers seeking to make a difference in their writing community.

The Quills Conference's annual banquet is also home to The Woolley Awards writing contest and the Quill Awards for published works.

Find out more about Quills at
www.leagueofutahwriters.com